THE
MYSTICAL
WOOD

THE MYSTICAL WOOD

JIL PLUMMER

The Mystical Wood

Copyright © 2019 Jil Plummer

Cover art by Nanaz White (original acrylic)

Published by Wittbits

www.wittbits.com

Jil Plummer

www.jilplummer.com

Printed in the United States of America

First Printing: October 2019

ISBN-13: 978-0-578-55036-7

ACKNOWLEDGMENTS

I am grateful to all the wonderful animals who have accompanied me through my life, especially my first horse Cleeve who taught me about unicorns. Of humans I thank Marjorie Witt with her generous advice and computer skills and my "Pendragons" writing group members who make each meeting a pleasure with their talent and encouragement.

In the medieval church the unicorn symbolized purity and the power of love-it would inherit the earth.

THE MYSTICAL WOOD

he Mystical Wood lies on the farthermost edge of the Faraway Forest and there all animals live in contentment from the Royal Unicorn to the tiny blind shrew. Trees grow special leaves for lions and tigers to eat and rain falls softly during the night, so each morning awakens new and fresh. Even in winter icicles drip honey and moss grows thick and warm for the animals to curl up in. The only human they know of comes in the mists of their dreams, and his name is Noah.

On a shiny April dawn, the thud of hooves sent squirrels scampering from their nest in the big oak tree. Beneath them swept the silvery body of the Unicorn, tossing diamonds of dew from the grass as he went, and they watched him gallop to the top of a hill and with a stiff- legged bounce, stop and look into the sunrise, his mane floating about him like a cloud. It settled to almost reach his knees as the sun struck golden lights from the horn on his forehead.

Back and forth his ears flickered as he listened to the wood's awakening. A thrush's song soared from the swaying top of a cedar while deep amid the trees a cuckoo sent out his two notes again and again. Young monkeys chattered and swung through branches as canaries tried to out-sing each other. Even the earth hummed as warmth sent ants scurrying and bees buzzing among crowds of bluebells.

With a swirl of his great tail and a toss of his head the Unicorn bounded downhill and raced through the meadow. Deer stopped grazing to watch him gallop through the sweeping sea of grass, and a startled hippopotamus popped the crust of his mud bath as the mist like blur flew over him. Ground animals dodged down holes until he had passed and then sat up quivering with excitement. The whole wood exploded with the joy of Spring.

The Unicorn stopped to graze, the sun warm along his back. A chipmunk's chitter broke the peace as it scampered toward him in a state of great agitation. Chipmunks were always excited about something so the Unicorn gave a welcoming snort and continued to pull at the lush clover. The chittering grew louder accompanied by much tail twitching until the Unicorn raised his head to look more carefully. A monkey now sat alongside also looking upset and, having captured the Unicorn's attention, the two darted back and forth coaxing him to follow. With a gusty sigh he decided to humor the little creatures.

They went down cool trails, monkey and chipmunk swooping through overhead branches. They passed an antelope and her calf whose dark, liquid eyes followed until they were out of sight. They crossed streams that laughed and chuckled from their very depths as the travelers drank, and branches stroked the strong white back and flanks of the Unicorn as he trod miles of springy ground. All day they travelled until, with a twinge of disquiet, the Unicorn realized they would soon reach the wood's edge. A strange noise came on the twilight breeze and he noticed that the animals he passed looked uneasy and fell in behind, forming a parade of shadowy shapes sliding through the dusk.

The sound grew closer and the Unicorn saw a change from bright colors to somber where the Mystical Wood ended and the Faraway Forest began. The animals moved quietly now, scarcely breathing. The two guides perched in a tree and peeked ahead from around the trunk. Feathery ferns leaned over the Unicorn as camouflage while he looked into the clearing and saw creatures the like of which he had never imagined. They could have belonged to the monkey tribe except for a strange difference in coat, and the Unicorn experienced wonder as he saw one remove a piece of hide, seemingly without pain, and hang it over a branch. Strange grunts came from their throats as with giant teeth they bit into a Sequoia until, with a moan, it crashed to the ground. It was the first sad sound the inhabitants of the wood had ever heard.

The Unicorn winced and turned back into the underbrush. All the animals followed, returning silently to their own places to ponder on the new feeling that had come over them. From then on many of the beasts who knew of the strange happenings at the edge of the wood passed there frequently out of curiosity, and as days came and went, they saw trees transformed into logs and then piled into something resembling a gigantic beaver lodge. Growing accustomed to the alien sounds some youngsters began to lose the wariness which had kept them from revealing their presence. The Unicorn did not know what fear was, but a warning in the wind told him to stay out of sight and he fretted at the indiscretions of others. Premonitions of danger disturbed his slumber and took away the sweetness of the grass.

BEFORE

"I sure won't be sorry to finish this job and get out of here." Joe squinted as he turned his coffee cup upside down to drain the last dregs into his mouth. "I don't reckon to envy those poor damn kids either, being shunted off here to the end of nowhere."

"Know what you mean." Tony answered. "S'pect they're on their way now. Think we'll have the place ready in time? Guess we got about three weeks."

Both men peered through darkness at the building in front of them. It was solid and square, three stories high with extremely small windows as if the place begrudged the least hint of sunshine squeezing inside. It seemed odd so many noble trees could make such a mean looking edifice.

Joe yawned and climbed into his sleeping bag. "Sure, we'll be ready." He watched a star fall and was glad he wasn't superstitious. "Hey Tony, what d'ya think those kids done so they built a special place like this for them? What about their folks? They won't be able to visit or nothin'."

"That's the idea. Been told it's the worst being sent here. Incorrigibles I've heard 'em called. Gang bangers, druggies, proven threats to society. Some psychiatrist's bright idea that isolation might cure them. Anyway, who'd want to visit them?"

"Ah Tony, come off it. They're all under sixteen, poor bastards. I reckon they're just unlucky to be chosen. Hey, if this school works, maybe we'll be building Juvi prisons in all sorts of out of the way places. Good money for us." Joe craned his neck and looked to make sure the other men were far enough away not to hear. "Hey Tony."

"What is it?"

"Have you ever seen anything strange since we come here?"

"Like what?"

"Well, I don't know, but remember when Bert said he was disappointed 'cause he didn't see deer or rabbits he could shoot? We didn't see nothing at all, remember? Well I've seen things. Not deer or rabbits but. well, promise you won't laugh?"

"I'm too sleepy to laugh. Spit it out, what did you see?"

"Things I've only seen in books. Like a kangaroo for instance, and once I could swear I saw a peacock. I didn't want to mention it in front of the others, they'd say I was nuts. Have you seen anything, Tony?"

A snore was his only answer. After a few moments Joe turned over and went to sleep. He couldn't see that Tony lay wide awake staring at the stars.

Weeks passed quickly for the small band of ten men, each hired for his particular skill. The building had three floors, the two uppers divided into cubicles and the ground one into five large rooms, entrance hall and kitchen. Tables and desks were made and stained, banisters smoothed, and a small forge beat out bars for each window. Outside storage sheds were built and a generator installed. The men worked long and hard but each night they slept well, filled with a sense of accomplishment.

Everything finished, on the final morning they took a last look at their handiwork and climbed into trucks for the long drive back to civilization. Joe felt strangely sad. He was surprised to find he had grown attached to the place even though each day the building had seemed more of a blasphemy to the peaceful surroundings. He had often gone to the edge of the clearing and looked into the untouched Wood feeling himself watched as he did so.

It was very different in there to the black forest they must drive through to get home. He wished he had the courage to explore farther but he never did.

The trucks rattled away and soon the new building stood alone wanting to be absorbed back into its beginnings, but that could not be. It had a purpose to fulfil.

The bolder animals came first. Monkeys opened doors and swung from light fixtures, calling to each other. Squirrels skittered up the banisters and explored cupboards while an Amazon parrot clung to an iron bar, pecking curiously at the window glass. A young pterodactyl flapped around the big hall enjoying the echo of its wings as a cobra reared to weave back and forth, watching.

Bigger animals followed. A giraffe nibbled the roof while a pride of lions wandered from room to room with round eyed kinkajous riding on their backs. A polar bear lounged in a bathtub rapidly filling with water turned on by an inquisitive koala bear and a flock of guinea hens screeched their way in and out of the cubicles.

Only the Unicorn was hesitant. He did not like to leave the Mystical Wood. Things were not the same outside; the ground was harder, and branches scratched. Finally, he ventured to the bottom of the steps and his nostrils flared as he breathed in the strange smells. He wheeled to walk around the building and as he did so his tail snagged on a corner of the stair, leaving behind a long silver strand.

He picked his way carefully through chunks of stone and mortar and then it started to rain. Not the gentle caressing rain he was used to but slashing knives of water that bit and stung his hide. The sound, as it drummed on the roof, sent animals scampering from inside and they whimpered with surprise at the unkind lashing of the storm. A wild rush began as they fled for the safety of their own wood and, once again within its comfort, they didn't look back but each went straight to its own coziest spot and curled up very small.

Only the Unicorn looked through rainbows back into the sodden clearing and saw a small mouse floating in a puddle with tiny pink feet curled tightly to its belly.

As it drifted around and around the Unicorn knew fear for the first time; it tingled along his backbone and sent him plunging deep into the heart of the Mystical Wood. Running and running he tried to shake off the memory of that first tiny death.

CHAPTER I

Two buses bounced, jarred and rattled along the unpaved road that crossed the plain. Two yellow dots, each wrapped in its own cloud of dust, and around them brown nothingness stretched to the horizon on four sides. Grit seeped through windows, clinging to the hot skin of the fifteen boys and four men in each vehicle. The men took turns driving and cursed each sweltering mile as it passed.

All society wanted was for these boys to be taken as far away as possible so that their criminal presences need never again be feared on the streets. This fear now paid large wages to the men who transported them to the distant, especially built prison school and who would keep them there in experimental isolation.

Every possible inch of bus was filled. Fine leather suitcases, still with stickers from cruises taken by affluent parents, squeezed in beside battered boxes and torn paper bags. The less a boy owned the closer he kept it to him. Many clutched all they possessed in their hands during the whole journey, even lugging it awkwardly on every trip to the stinking toilet in the compartment behind the rear seats.

Among belongings of men and boys were boxes of provisions; cans of vegetables, sacks of rice and spaghetti, beans, blankets, towels and soap, books and pencils. Everything that could keep the school going until more supplies came by helicopter. In the first bus, somewhere, a carton of apples slowly rotted and pervaded the atmosphere with their sweet stench.

Gabby, fourteen years old, hunched his scrawny body in disgust as he watched the kid across the aisle vomit. His own stomach surged. He turned to the window feeling sweat trickle down his spine. Neither blood nor barf nor spilled guts affected leaders and this bunch of losers may not know it yet, but he was theirs. They'd soon be doing anything he told them to. They'd respect the hell out of him and that was all Gabby wanted in a life he took for granted would be short. Most were in his neighborhood- by gun or knife-maybe poison. He eyed his fellow passengers. Hell, one of them might try to poison him some day. He'd have to watch out. A paper bag rustled in his ear and, not looking at the man who offered it, he dug out a sandwich. He devoured it in three bites. As he licked his fingers he wondered if every sandwich was peanut butter or if he just kept getting them while everyone else ate salami or cheese. He craned to see if his suspicion was true but the others had eaten as fast as he had. All except one, a slight dark boy who still nibbled delicately, savoring each bite. Gabby watched with disgust, despising the boy whose type he had seen roaming the nighttime streets of his neighborhood. Faggot, he hissed and turned to the drab parade of dust outside.

His thoughts, caught in the engine's roar, invented rhythm. Rap chanted and crescendoed in his head. Unconsciously he reached inside his shirt and pulled out two polished drumsticks. They were short and fit snugly in the hidden leather pouch he wore against his ribs. At first the strap chafed his skin, but he had grown to like the irritation that reminded him of his prize possessions and of Jeff, the only friend he'd ever had. Just a homeless guy who sat on the pavement and played drums. Gabby had loved to listen. It set his feet jumping and lifted his heart to somewhere he'd never been before. Jeff would talk to him about music and places he'd played and people he'd known before. He never said before what and it didn't seem right to ask. Then one day he gave Gabby the little pouch with the drumsticks. "If you got rhythm you always got somewheres to go when things get rough," he'd said.

Soon after that Jeff's bit of pavement became empty. Day after day-nothing. Someone said he'd gotten hit by a car and the dead people's van had taken him away. Gabby chose to believe he'd been offered a gig in some uptown club.

The drumsticks, reminder of his one friend, had become Gabby's most valuable possession and the challenge of keeping them secret had led to all sorts of tricky maneuvers since his imprisonment thirteen months before. He had overcome each problem. Each another small battle won against the enemy.

Tappety-tap they went on the metal top of the seat ahead of him. Tappety-tap-tap. Louder. The roar of the bus became the hum of voices in a smoky room where Gabby sat amid flashing lights surrounded by Jeff's imaginary band. Eyes half closed he rocked as his sticks beat wildly.

"Shuddup, dammit!"

Spray from a mouth twisted with annoyance sprinkled Gabby's frantic hands. Slowly a glaring red face became real, breaking his dream.

"Shuddup!" The squawk came again.

Gabby's wrists locked. He glared into the face turned to him from the seat ahead. Quick as a rattler, he shifted the sticks into one hand and with the other reached for the nose above the distorted mouth. One twist and the boy screamed, facing forward in agony, hands covering his face.

Gabby beat a triumphant tattoo and stuffed the sticks back into their hiding place. He hoped the others had seen what happened to whoever smart assed him. His reputation had already spread during the journey and most already treated him with wary respect. Things were going well.

CHAPTER II

G abby had spent his life in the big city world of street gangs and after Jeff left, he had concentrated on fighting his way up to be second in command of the "Sinners".

He had no father. His mother hated him for being in the way, as she often expressed while locking him in the cupboard when she went out at night. Now on this new turf he swore nothing on earth would stop him. He would be the toughest, meanest of all bad asses, that's what it took to be warlord of a gang. You had to be the baddest, then you got respect. He stroked the knife scar on his arm. Actually, it had been a very small slash in his one knife fight, but someone had told him you could make a good scar if you kept picking and fussing at a cut as it tried to heal. He had worked diligently on this one causing a dramatic advertisement of past battles. He couldn't afford tattoos but scars, like broken teeth, were to be envied. He'd had broken teeth too, but they turned out to be baby ones so that mark of prestige had gone, to be replaced by strong white ones of which he was secretly proud. He wished he were taller but with all his sharp angles, quick temper and the fighting moves he'd learned off TV he didn't need to fight to gain respect, just one look usually did it. The only problem had been that his voice had

11

not matured with the rest of him which had made people look surprised and then laugh when they heard him speak –however the murder had fixed that.

Yeah, I've got this bunch under control, he thought slumping down in the seat, now I'll just have the other bus load to whip into shape when we get there. Then I'll choose who I want for my gang to do whatever I tell 'em to do. I'm goin' to run this whole fucking place. And when they let me back out onto the streets I'll have respect and not just be second in the Sinners anymore.

He thought about it for a while and fell into a doze.

Hours passed though there was nothing to prove it. God he was bored. Dust still swirled and Gabby wondered if it was the same they carried with them all the time. Perhaps it was a plot so they couldn't see where they were going.

After being in the remand home for a whole long year Gabby had been pleased when told he was to be moved. He'd thought any change would be better. Now he wasn't so sure.

He winced the muscles in his buttocks to relieve the aching stiffness but nothing helped. He figured he'd never be able to sit down again when this was over. Never. He wiped the window with his bare arm and found he could see farther than he expected. Pressing his nose to the glass he peered and almost imagined something dark loomed ahead. He watched it get closer and closer.

Gabby blinked. The sun disappeared and great tree trunks pressed in as a forest swallowed them. Where were the familiar city streets and dangers he understood? He sank lower. I won't know what T.V. shows there are, which teams win what games, the latest rap artist. This last sent a shudder through him and he hunkered tighter in his corner forcing himself to replace the sound of the bus's engine with the grinding roar of garbage trucks and his taste buds to savor the flavor of half eaten steak scavenged from cans outside neighborhood restaurants. Gabby's insides felt light and swoopy and scared for a moment. He closed his eyes pretending to sleep.

A change of pace snapped him upright to see everyone looking intently up the road ahead. Grasping the metal hand hold on the seat in front he balanced, half standing, and saw a truck, then behind it another and a third, all filled with men and tools hurtling towards them and on past back toward civilization. As they went the men grinned and waved looking curiously in at the boys. Then they were gone. With every sinew Gabby yearned to go with them and his eyes strained to follow long after the road was empty.

"It won't be forever kid. You'll see it all again someday." One of the guards towered beside Gabby in the aisle.

All grown-ups were liars. When he had been small and ignorant, he had trusted some of them. They'd held out their arms and talked fine words about goodness and God, and then he'd gone home and repeated some of it to his mother, the overpowering loud woman who was out most of the time and when she was home made the room they lived in the center of a continuous storm.

When he'd said the words to her, quoting in his piping baby voice, she had swiped him across the face and stirred the storm into a hurricane.

Grown-ups hadn't helped him then nor later when the gangs bullied him. Adults faded like puffs of smoke only to reappear with fingers avidly pointing at his first trouble with the law. By then he knew there were no such things as friends. He was all he had and he made it be enough. Now this jerk stood looking at him. Expects me to think how nice and understanding he is. Stupid soft bastard.

It seemed a long time before the presence moved on and then with a shuddering sigh Gabby relaxed, one hand resting on the comfort of his drumsticks.

The atmosphere inside the bus was quiet and lonely as men and boys realized they had seen the last of any world they knew for a long, long time.

Two more days and nights they travelled the rough forest road, now barely a track, stopping only for short breaks to stretch their legs and eat tasteless food stored in now warm freezer chests. It was a never-ending nightmare. Gabby felt he couldn't bear another minute but didn't know what he could do about it. The aches, the sounds, the smells and the boredom were unbearable. If he could have died, he would have, but he couldn't, so he just sat and seethed.

Once they stopped beside a pond and everyone but Gabby stripped and jumped in with loud shouts and splashing. Brown scum floated on the surface from grimy bodies and though Gabby longed to feel cool water wash away the itchiness that crawled all over him he didn't want to reveal his drumsticks, so impatiently paced the clearing showing annoyance at the delay.

It was on the afternoon of the sixth interminable day that tiger-stripes of sunlight slashed and darted through the bus signaling a change. Before the passengers could rouse from their near comatose states the bus burst into a large field and the brightness of mid-day tore at eyes accustomed to forest gloom. Between blinks Gabby saw the solid block of a building and the bars black across narrow windows.

THE UNICORN

The Unicorn, forced by a nagging compulsion, again ventured to look out at the clearing with its ugly pile of logs. Nothing had changed but he felt the wind hold its breath and noted the dark clouds lurking overhead.

With a shudder he turned back into the wood and sank down on a mossy patch of sunlight. Green scents ruffled his nostrils and a warm breeze tugged at his forelock, pulling him toward sleep. Each time his head drooped, and his chin touched the ground he would jolt awake and listen - he didn't know what for.

Eventually he dozed, drifting back through his memories until they faded into some that were not really his and he saw the strange two-legged shape whose eyes looked at him with great compassion. It seemed to warn against others of its own kind-and it called them men.

The vision told the Unicorn to prepare to fight; but creatures of the wood knew nothing about fighting. As though he knew this, the stranger rested his hand for an instant on the noble white forehead, wearing all the while an expression of such deep sadness that the Unicorn awoke trembling and leaped to his feet. A loud hubbub surrounded him and he saw that a murder of crows had flown in from the Faraway Forest, cawing and flapping among the branches. Suddenly they hushed and all focus was on the rumbling sound which came closer and closer.

CHAPTER III

The bus shuddered to a halt. Every boy scrambled to collect his belongings: pushing and shoving, ignoring shouts to stay in their seats. Gabby alone stayed in place, stretching and yawning as though still half asleep. The bus door squealed open. In one quick move he was on his feet, knapsack over his shoulder, surprising those in the way of his sharp elbows and well-placed kicks.

He jumped outside and strode away from the shouts and fighting away from the fetid atmosphere; ignoring the bellowed commands to wait.

At last he stopped and stared into the face of the building. It stared back, blank and expressionless.

Ha, Gabby thought, you think to imprison me. To smother me in your guts. But think again! I'm gonna to be boss here. You'll see.

One of the muscled guards had crossed the field and now grabbed his arm. Gabby complied but jerked loose when they reached where the others lined up after tumbling, jumping or being shoved down the bus steps. The men puffy and red faced stood in front and everyone looked toward the track as the nose of the second bus emerged from the trees.

The two vehicles had never stopped at the same times and places during the whole journey and now, as this new arrival let out its passengers, every eye evaluated them and tried to guess why they were there. Each hoped it wasn't for as vicious a crime as his own.

Gabby didn't even think about it. He knew from hearing people talk at his trial that he was considered a monster. That's what the papers said in wonderful, blazing headlines: "Monster Son Slaughters Mother." It was all the blood that upset people but the notoriety made him special and gave him prestige among all who mattered.

He thrust his hands into his jeans hip pockets. Hell, what makes them so important we have to stand out here like a dumb welcoming committee? With studied nonchalance Gabby stared into space, chewing the same piece of gum he had set out with six days before. He figured he'd better save everything he could from outside. He might never get a replacement and, stuffing it carefully in his cheek when he ate, the gum, although long since tasteless, had survived.

The eight men talked while the two groups of boys waited, a wary distance between them. With a shuffle of papers and poised pencil the Warden, who had traveled in the second bus, looked them over, then began to call roll.

Names, always names, Gabby thought. If a name's not answered will they hop back in the bus and roar off looking for its owner? Not likely. More probable they'd be glad to get rid of us. He knew how they thought and hoped they could see the contempt he felt for them. They'd be gung-ho for a while but then they'd slack off. They always did.

Guards, teachers, it made no difference, they were all the same. Even mothers. Gabby quickly flushed that word out of his consciousness.

Names and replies droned on and Gabby checked his stance. Shoulders hunched like he'd heard bikers such as Hell's Angels' always were; jaw set and square, chomping gum in measured cadence, feet firm and wide apart. In his mind he was Terminator in the latest remake of the old movie.

Silence. His name rang out a second time. "Arthur Siskin." He felt like killing anyone who called him that. In fact, he almost had a few times. And Siskin! The derivations he'd been called had probably helped make him, from earliest childhood, the vicious fighter he was.

Maybe if his Ma had known the name of his father, he could have had a different last name. Bitch!

"Arthur Siskin!"

Everyone stared but Gabby's jaws just kept chewing as he watched a crow swoop overhead to sit on a corner of the roof and scream at them.

"Answer when your names called, Boy." The Warden's nose flushed red and he shaded his eyes to see Gabby better.

A man from the first bus leaned over and tapped the roll taker's shoulder. "The kid can't talk." His whisper was loud so everyone could hear.

"Never?"

"Not that we know about."

Even the crow was quiet as everyone inspected Gabby.

Take a good look you bastards. You'll soon find fists speak louder than words by a long shot. Carelessly he spat onto the grass and then squinted at the sky as roll call continued.

Final names were called. Gabby let his gaze slide over to the other group where his eyes slammed against a pair of cold white ones in a narrow pock-marked face.

Trouble. Gabby's fists clenched in his pockets and his feet tingled ready to spring and kick. Two pairs of eyes glared and hated each other for a few moments until Gabby unlocked his, spat again and coolly swaggered after the others who had begun to move in the direction of the building. It was good to know his enemy so soon, to have one solid familiar thing in this lonesome place. He got a chin full of hair as the kid in front of him stopped short and a shout from up ahead brought the men running past to pound up the steps and into the building. They talked excitedly among themselves and behind them the boys craned and shoved eager to see what was going on. Over heads Gabby saw a big room strewn with broken furniture and debris while water streamed down a wide staircase.

A guard splashed through on his way from the floor above. "It was a bathtub. Workman must have left it running, but who did all this?"

The men stood around looking perplexed. "They're not supposed to be any humans within a hundred miles of here," said one. "I don't like it."

For Pete's sake get on with it, Gabby thought. Keeping us all jammed up here. Hell, what's the problem? It doesn't look much more torn up than most of the places I've lived in.

Being so packed together smelled like the bus again and made him nauseous so he turned and pushed back down the steps where he rested his elbows on the lowest balustrade. If only he could get rid of the bus's motion and the roar of it from his head.

Automatically he inspected the bleak front of the building for escape routes. Small barred windows and only one big door with locks on it that meant business. Not much to work on there. Three other sides waited to be checked. Idiot! Gabby mentally kicked himself. Who'd be stupid enough to run away into a million miles of forest? Gabby shuffled the bag he had set between his sneakers and lowered his head, half shutting his eyes as the sun warmed his neck reminding him how tired he was.

A tiny sparkle insinuated itself into his consciousness and he bent to inspect it. Deep in a crack something glimmered with a strange luminous intensity, seeming to flow like a trickle of quicksilver out and down the side of the post to the ground. It swayed gently leaving a glowing shadow image with each movement and when Gabby put out his hand it flowed across his palm like a cool sliver of mist.

Gabby closed his fingers and tore it loose so as to look more closely. Just an old hair. He'd hoped for more. It was weird though, sort of like music he had never heard that aroused feelings he had never felt. His gaze clung to it and a thought drifted to the edge of his mind and hovered just out of reach; something important.

"Move it, man." Boys pushed him out of the way as they charged up the steps and in through the door. Gabby quickly wrapped the hair around his hand, clutched his bag, kicked the shins of the kid who crowded him, and entered the damp smelling building.

"Siskin. Cubicle twelve. First floor. Unpack, sit on your bed and wait."

Gabby followed the man's directions, climbing the slimy stairs. A long hall stretched away to his left and on either side mold-green curtains hung limply, pretending to give privacy to the cubicles behind. Each cloth moved lethargically as he passed looking for his number. He paused by the opening to a large shower room which tempted him with thoughts of warm water sluicing away the grime and lingering stench of the journey, but he moved on.

Number twelve. Right at the end. Like a cave. They'll have a tough time sneaking up on me here. He pushed through the curtain, closed it carefully so no space showed on either side, put his bag on the floor, and then looked around. It was a small area but big enough for the narrow metal cot and white chest of drawers it held. It was his own private place and that was what counted. With a sigh he flumphed down onto the striped mattress and crossed his arms behind his head. Halfway along the wall a wavy mirror reflected his feet in a strangely shriveled way. Gabby watched his sneakers accordion as he moved and played with the image for a few moments then he strained his head back to look at the stingy barred window high above him. Jumping up onto the bed he found that he could just stretch to look out and see part of a playing field and beyond that trees. Better than the last place which had no window at all.

Back on the floor, he folded to his knees beside the bed. The floor was dark, shiny and cold looking. Thank goodness winter was past. Pressing carefully with his hands he felt from board to board until one gave a tremor and he knew that with a little effort he would be able to pry it up to make a hiding place. Just in case he ever needed one.

Gabby stood up and took in the whole space with its cot and dresser with drawers that worked. Even a water jug on top. All this was his. Wow! It was like winning the lottery. A place of his own! He'd never had that before.

He dumped the clothes from his bag onto the bed: Jeans, two regulation blue shirts, socks and two sets of underwear lay in a tangle. A toothbrush followed, clunking onto the floor. Gabby stuffed everything into drawers and wondered what to do next.

A glimmer caught his eye and he was surprised to see the strange hair still wound around his palm. He untwisted it and let one end float to the floor. The meagre dusting of sunlight that struggled into the room made the strand quiver as though alive. Gabby strained to understand the secrets it was trying to whisper to him.

The long drive must have made him weak minded! Approaching footsteps startled him into bundling the hair into a tight ball and stuffing it into the hidden pouch with his drumsticks. Then he lay on the mattress and feigned sleep.

CHAPTER IV

Thump. Something landed on Gabby's stomach, knocking the wind out of him. Quick as a coiled spring he reared up into the grinning face of the guard who watched from the doorway. The grin grew wider and Gabby hated it. With a vicious swing of his arm he knocked the bedclothes which had been dumped on him to the floor.

"Time to make your bed, boy. Sheet on the bottom, blankets on top."

Gabby glared and felt the skin draw tight over his cheeks.

"When you've done that get downstairs to help clean up the place. You hear me?"

Stiff as a ramrod Gabby glared his hatred and the man seemed stuck on the end of his gaze like a fly on a pin. The beady bug eyes blinked, and the man started to back out through the curtain but stopped halfway with it draped foolishly over his head. "Say, you're the dumb one, aren't you?" This time the guard looked at Gabby as though he were the insect. "Can't you talk, kid, or is it just that you won't?"

Gabby loathed him more than ever and for a moment longer they stared at each other, then the man snorted and ran his hand under his nose. "Have it your own way but hurry up and get downstairs."

The curtain dropped and Gabby was alone.

As his anger waned, he mulled over the guard's last question. Can I speak? He couldn't answer himself. He honestly didn't know. He really meant to try, maybe in the john or someplace, but whenever he got himself ready, he would remember that even there someone might just hear him. And what if he did still have that puny high voice?

He didn't know why it mattered but it did. He had talked fine in that kid's voice before his mother died, but then he found silence was the only answer he had for the police, lawyers and guards who had been in his life ever since. No one ever laughed at him now. In fact, his silence seemed to spook kids - and the "look" of course. He'd perfected that in front of a mirror, and it made most people decide to do things his way. He got up now and gave it a try. The uneven glass made him appear even more threatening.

Might as well make the bed. He glanced toward the hall. But not because you said to, Pig!

Something crashed downstairs. Laughter. Far off shouting. Then more laughter.

Before he could think Gabby was loping down the hall. At the head of the stairs he paused to run his fingers the wrong way through his kinky black hair; then he sauntered down.

Kids bustled everywhere, sweeping, polishing and hammering. Gabby stopped on the bottom step to watch and immediately an empty bucket and a mop were thrust at him.

"Second floor bathroom," someone said and was gone. Gabby's impulse to disobey the order and drop his load was overruled by realization that at least upstairs he'd be out of sight, so he hung the bucket on the end of his mop handle and started back up.

One kid was on his knees polishing the top step. Gabby, climbing, toward him despised the delicate body so different from his own tough, stringy one. 'Beauty' they'd called him. What a name! Gabby grinned as his imagination saw how the tin of polish the boy held would shine and bounce as it rolled down the stairs after he'd kicked it from the sissy's hand. He could already hear the guards bellow at the faggot's clumsiness.

23

Gabby climbed faster in anticipation but suddenly the can was flying toward him, tossing chunks of wax, clanking and spinning. First Gabby saw Beauty's startled expression, then the solid, dough-faced boy with the pale eyes who descended, with slow deliberation, in the very center of the staircase.

Adrenalin flooded Gabby in anticipation of this first confrontation with his enemy, stiffening his back and bringing an excited tingle to his skin. His fists whitened around the mop handle as he also moved to the middle of each stair, eyes fixed unblinking on the colorless ones ahead. Both boys stopped, stiff legged, bristling like terriers, blocking each other's way.

"Move, boy." Whiteyes' voice was high and nasal.

Gabby screwed his face into the "look" mustering all the menace he could.

The pale eyes didn't flinch.

From the silence Gabby knew all the boys watched and above, on the edge of his vision, he was aware of Beauty's long lashed gaze, anxious and frightened. Gabby gave a few slow chews on his gum. He watched the pulse in his opponent's pock-marked cheek and was ready when Whiteyes lunged toward him with a hard-heavy shoulder. Gabby sprang aside, foot lashing out, striking below the knee, collapsing it so he saw his enemy tumble past, crashing downstairs after the tin of polish.

Gabby didn't look back. Just continued on his way carrying his bucket high like a banner, his heart thumping with triumph.

"Thank you."

He half stopped in surprise when he heard Beauty's whisper. Silly bastard thinks I did it for him. That'll be the day. Gabby walked jauntily on down the hall.

The bathroom was big with three tubs and a row of showers and another of basins. The tile floor was covered with water and the place smelled like the basement of a tenement. It was almost dark and Gabby waited, listening for any sound of rats. Reasonably satisfied there were none he took off his shoes, set them in a sink, and slopped around bare foot enjoying the echoes his mop made banging against the fixtures. He could almost make a tune. A low

24

hum joined the clangor and lights flashed on. It was as though he had removed a wide brimmed hat and he was relieved to be able to see into the corners and find there really were no lurking insects or rodents different to the ones at home.

He wondered if the water in the taps was warmer than the mess on the floor. His feet ached and they looked wan and puckered there below him.

Leaning over a bathtub Gabby hoicked the plug from the drain. The tub's inch of stagnant water didn't move. He looked more closely. Maybe someone had hidden something down there. Dope or jewels stashed by whoever had wrecked the place. He'd hidden stuff in the drain of his bathtub back home-it was the safest place - no one ever used the tub except maybe to store papers or potatoes. Plunging his hand into the water he scrabbled with his fingers before pulling out a wad of course, matted white hair. Jeese! Must have been weird people bathing here. Washing fur coats maybe. He pulled the wad apart letting the pieces flutter to the floor where they tickled his feet and reminded him of his original purpose. Shaking the last few hairs from his hands he turned the hot water tap as far as it would go.

Water gushed and boomed into the tub and soon steam billowed.

Gabby rolled up his cuffs and climbed in, lowering his bony bottom to sit on the porcelain edge. Balancing, he held his feet under the hot water letting it flow between his toes and around his ankles. He closed his eyes to concentrate on the pleasure of it. When he opened them, it was like being in a dense fog shut away from the world. His toes rose to the mouth of the faucet sending spray all over himself and then he directed water to different targets until the walls ran and the ceiling dripped.

"What the hell's going on here?" An arm reached over Gabby's shoulder and turned the water off, surprise nearly toppling him from his perch.

The only sound now was a dismal faint trickle and Gabby refused to acknowledge the man who stood behind him.

"Look kid, you're not starting off too well you know." The voice struggled to sound low and reasonable. "It'll be best all round if you understand some things. If you don't rock the boat it'll be easy for you here, we'd just as soon forget you kids as much as possible, but if we have to, we can get tough. It's up to you."

Gabby closed out the words and sat, stiff, ignoring.

It didn't matter what they said, he knew what they thought.

As soon as grown-ups set eyes on him Gabby knew that, man or woman, they hated him and pinned all the worst crimes in the neighborhood on his account. Of course, that gave him all the more prestige with his gang and got him to be second in command so he didn't complain, but now and again he wished…. oh well….

He twirled his toes through water that slurped noisily down the drain aware of how much the man longed to grab his shoulders and shake him. Gabby squared them, daring him.

The voice began again, harsh this time and louder with each word. "You just get to work and dry this place up. There'll be no supper until the building's in order so 'lest you want to starve you'd better get to moving."

Gabby gave a resounding, smacking chew on his gum and grinned to hear the angry clomp of retreating boots. Slowly he swung his legs around to the floor and stood up. He began swabbing. Back and forth. Squeeze the water out. Back and forth. The room seemed to stretch forever, and he saw himself reflected in a myriad shiny faucets and showerheads; an army of skinny black gnomes, forever destined to clean the world's outhouses.

Wet all over from sweat or steam his arms ached and the place seemed to be crowding in on him. His mop banged against the wall. The end-at last. A final squeeze. He dumped the dirty water down a shower drain and headed for the door, gnomes joining and parting as he walked back up the still dripping room. In the hall outside he put on his shoes and his stomach rumbled. Please let that bell mean food!

CHAPTER V

Other boys joined him heading downstairs and then they thundered along the halls bumping and shoving like a herd of cattle. When they reached the dining room they spread out and scuffled for places at each of the three green, oilcloth covered tables where guards and teachers were already positioned behind steaming bowls of beans and spinach.

"Pass your plates," the man at Gabby's table ordered.

When Gabby's returned to him loaded with chicken, mashed potatoes and veggies he forgot everything in the absolute bliss of eating something other than peanut butter sandwiches.

For twelve minutes the room was completely quiet but for the steady clatter of cutlery.

Gabby speared the last bean and gulped his second glass of reconstituted milk. With a sigh he shoved back his chair and looked around. Time to start planning. His eyes roved from face to face; it wasn't going to be easy picking the right guys for his gang. Some looked awful puny and younger than the twelve-year lower age limit. That black kid looks strong and mean---he thought- and maybe the one next to him, but not that little punk with glasses. Then he remembered the small kid with a squint who was best with a chain of all the "Angels" until he got caught in a robbery and sent away. Choosing sure was going to be tough. Travelling from boy to boy Gabby's eyes met those of Beauty and moved quickly away from his timid half-smile. Not him for certain. Suddenly all he wanted was sleep.

Tink, tink. The sound of a spoon hitting glass drew everyone's attention toward the middle table where the Warden now leaned vulture-like toward them. He cleared his throat. "I'm Warden Dean and as you know I'm in charge of our little group here. Our only physical contact with the outside world will be the helicopter which will come once a month with mail and supplies. Apart from that we're on our own." He paused to clear his throat again. "Now I know none of you would be stupid enough to try to escape but just in case it had crossed anyone's mind you should know that the buses are up on blocks with the engines dismantled and the forest is mighty big and full of hungry animals, I've been told. So however you look at it your chances would be pretty slim." He smiled, looking pleased with himself.

Gabby, struggling to stay awake, stared stonily at the man's Adam's apple. He can't say one thing that would interest me, he thought, not one thing. Nothing that could scare me neither. If I want to escape I will. Gabby's seat ached, not yet recovered from the bus ride, and he shifted causing the bench to squeak. Get with it you old windbag. Gabby fixed his eyes on the man and willed him to finish.

"Let's all pull together and make this a decent community so..."

Gabby's message obviously wasn't getting through. His eyes stung. He'd have to switch to more practical methods. With an imperceptible movement of his hips he made the bench groan and as the Warden's voice ran on and on Gabby interrupted with a nagging punctuation. Squeak. Squeak

The voice grew fidgety as the boys' attention wavered and the man's eyes darted, searching.

Gabby, still as a stone above the waist, watched with interest the flush that began at the beaklike nose and spread across the Warden's narrow cheeks.

Squeak.

"Tomorrow you will all rise at the sound of the first bell, dress and descend to breakfast..."

Squeak.

"Then you will be told the routine you will follow strictly every day thereafter and I want..."

Squeak.

Giggles were spreading.

Warden glared around the room as though he could see inside each boy's head. Gabby stared back impassively.

"Right, on the double up to bed."

Release startled the boys into action and with a wild scramble they fled the room. Gabby galloped two stairs at a time knocking others out of his way. The game he had played with the Warden left him exhilarated and he knew it was points in his favor with the others.

Once in the lonely, cold hours he awoke and sleepily heard a jungle show on T.V. But there was no T.V. out here. The roars and squeals continued and he pulled the blankets over his head. He'd think about it in the morning.

THE UNICORN

The animals prowled nervously throughout the night, crowding the darkness with roars, squeals and the quavering laugh of hyenas, but by first light all was quiet and the Unicorn stood wreathed in mist at the edge of the clearing.

The new arrivals were awakening. He heard strange bursts of sound and then came unfamiliar smells that made his lip curl. Occasionally one or two creatures broke away from the building but as they stayed far from the wood the Unicorn's fears eased.

Nothing changed, thrushes warbled, branches shivered with morning ecstasy and the purr of a nearby leopard lent warmth to the sun.

The Unicorn sighed and relaxed.

CHAPTER VI

The wakeup bell jarred on and on, reaching along the halls and behind the green curtains.

Startled from deep sleep Gabby shot upward until the lingering ache in his buttocks reminded him of where he was, and he lay back wishing he could sleep forever.

Lights flashed on. Eyelids squeezed tight against the brightness, Gabby pulled on his jeans and slouched out into the hall to join other somnambulistic figures wandering toward the washroom. The water was cold on his face and it wasn't until he was well soaked that he remembered his towel still lay on his bed. No problem. He hoisted his T-shirt over his face and patted the wetness into it. He did it casually as though that was the way he always dried himself. It looked tough, but as the shirt clung clammily to his stomach on the way back to his cubicle, he decided to remember the towel next time.

Critically he watched his reflection in the mirror as he combed his hair back, then sharply forward into a deep wave, sneered then, pleased with the effect, carefully strapped on his drumstick pouch which had lain hidden under his mattress. Gabby pushed through his curtain as the second bell rang.

31

The morning air was brisk, and it took a conscious effort for Gabby to stop his teeth from chattering. He rubbed the goose bumps from his arms so by the time he reached the stairs he looked unaffected by the chill or anything else for that matter; which is how a leader should look.

He joined the rest of the boys in the downstairs hall and sat on the lowest stair whistling quietly as he inspected his hands. He ignored it when the boys stopped muttering and the sound of heavy footsteps approached.

In the silence Gabby bit off a fingernail, spat it out, then casually looked up.

"Now we have your attention perhaps you'll join the others and we can get on with things," said the older man who had travelled in Gabby's bus and now towered over him.

A guard watched from against the far wall.

Gabby slowly stood and strolled over to slouch against the opposite window frame.

"Good morning, boys." A teacher climbed onto the vacated step. "Listen carefully while I announce your daily curriculum."

"Our what?" A voice that might have been Whiteyes' caused a ripple of laughter.

The man ignored the interruption. "After breakfast you will return upstairs and tidy your cubicles."

The boys groaned in disgust.

"Classes will begin after a half hour of calisthenics outside. Twelve o'clock will be lunch after which you will attend your designated trade class. Look for it on the bulletin board. After four you are free to amuse yourselves on the playing field until supper at five thirty. The evening will be either spent studying in the main hall or you must retire to your cubicles."

He spoke faster as he went along hardly pausing for breath as though afraid the accompanying moans and groans might take over.

Gabby hardly noticed the words. He was more interested in the boys around him. What had they done to deserve being sent here?

Some looked too young to be capable of more than pinching something from a Dollar store but when he saw their eyes there was no youth there. Even when the mouth smiled no laughter reached farther and Gabby recognized the expression as similar to his own in the mirror each day. Others in the group were almost like grown men with hard mean faces, always looking for a fight. Only one boy was completely different. Gabby studied the pale skin and resigned expression of Beauty. It carried a mixture of timidity and defiance, cockiness and despair.

Gabby turned back to the teacher who was almost shouting.

"You will each be assigned duties which will be changed every few weeks. There'll be laundry, helping the cook, mopping halls, yard work etc. etc. so check the board for the list tomorrow."

"What about weekends?" someone called out.

"Duties and homework will keep you occupied most of the time and there will be a church service on Sunday. Now we'll file in for breakfast but first ..."

He was too late. Already the boys headed as one for the narrow passage to the dining room.

The burly guard blocked their way. "Hold it!" he bellowed while the teacher scurried up beside him.

"I want to read out the order of seating in the dining room. Remember and keep to it. Understood? Table number one; Anderson, Bramley..."

Gabby wondered who he'd be stuck next to. Not that it mattered, he'd mostly ignore whoever it was. Years before when he'd met a new kid he'd wonder if they'd be friends. Now he only had enemies and followers. Friends made you weak, took away a bit of yourself and besides, you couldn't trust anyone but yourself. Gabby had found that out long ago.

He elbowed more space for himself and wished they could get moving. He hated being crowded.

Five minutes later Gabby dug into a heaping bowl of oatmeal. He enjoyed eating almost anything. Food was something to be relished to the last available bite. Too many times during his fourteen years he had gone to bed empty having searched every corner of the apartment for something to eat and found nothing. It had taught him to collect what he could on his way home, from garbage cans or unwary shop attendants. Even when he didn't need it he hoarded whatever he could get his hands on. Now, filled to bursting, he stuffed a piece of bread under his shirt.

He sauntered upstairs deep in thought, letting other kids run past. He wished he still had his gum which had dissolved during his first real meal and would have helped now as he worried at something he'd noticed about Whiteyes on their first meeting; that faint sheen on his cheeks and upper lip. Was he really mature enough to shave?

Gabby automatically stuck out a foot and tripped a boy who ran too close.

He had verified his suspicion last night at their confrontation, but the thrill of victory had driven it from his mind until he'd seen Whiteyes again this morning. That washed out bastard had whiskers! Very few but what an envied mark of manhood. Gabby moved faster and when he got behind his curtain bounded to the wavy mirror, leaning close, willing his eyes to confirm growth on his own face, however faint. Shit, not a sprout.

Dejected, Gabby sat on the edge of his bed then suddenly an idea sent him to his feet reaching to run his fingers along the top of the doorway. They came away covered with dust and very carefully he patted it over the imaginary beard line of his face. He pressed it in and dabbed off the excess on the corner of a towel. On his already dark complexion the smudgy upper lip and shadowy chin really did look almost like whiskers. Not just pale fuzz like Whiteyes had either. Gabby grinned.

A bell jangled through his satisfied musings and, after quickly heaving the covers over his bed, he joined the others on the playing field, moving onto the wheel of routine which rolled into the future with no sign of a break.

CHAPTER VII

The teacher of the first class faced the sweaty boys who had just poured into his room. One by one he asked them a math problem, ticking a little book at each answer. Gabby knew he was testing them, finding who was smart and who wasn't. The thirty boys were to be divided into two groups, advanced and backward, and Gabby was going to make sure he was in the former. He knew he was smarter than anyone and he'd prove it, but first he'd have some fun.

The chunky kid next to him didn't have a clue when it came his turn and Gabby watched while he stuttered and struggled, finally blurting out any old number just to get the teacher off his back. The man wrote in his book and turned to Gabby.

"All right, Siskin. Can you tell us the answer?"

Gabby stared impassively forward.

"Siskin, what's the answer to this equation? Come on, boy, we don't have all day."

Gabby scraped his chair back.

"Sit still, boy, and tell me the answer if you know it."

Gabby just looked at him.

Growing white around his mouth the teacher strode up the aisle and stopped, looking down on Gabby's head. His voice came out low and tight. "Siskin, I don't want trouble but so help me I'll send you to the Warden if you don't speak us. Do you know the answer?"

Gabby half rose from his seat and the hand that pushed him back almost turned the chair over with the force of it.

"Where the hell do you think you're going?"

A snigger burst from the watching class, and then another.

As the teacher turned angrily toward them a red-haired boy shouted, "Gabby can't speak. He has to write it."

The teacher seemed to shrink. Then with a sigh he waved Gabby to the blackboard.

Gabby grinned around the room and strode to the front where he scratched the answer in bold square figures, breaking the chalk on the last stroke. By the glazed look in the teacher's eyes he knew he was correct and loped smugly back to his desk.

That was the last time a teacher forgot Gabby's disability as they called it, and the classes soon fell into a boring routine. Afternoons weren't too bad as Gabby found the wood-working class to which he was assigned almost enjoyable. The knife, with its especially short blade to make it useless as a weapon, felt good sliding through chunks of wood and although the boys were supposed to make things like spoons or bowls Gabby found himself an out of the way corner and whittled objects he knew, like miniature fire hydrants or a small wooden drum. Things that reminded him of outside.

If he went slowly completing his morning assignment, he could miss most of the exercise class and as he mopped the halls or washed dishes, he planned his strategy. However, soon he began to worry. For all his thinking he was no further toward assembling his gang than on the first day. He must do something. But what? However, much he puzzled he couldn't figure how to get started. If he could talk it would be different. The boys respected and feared him, he knew that. Even Whiteyes gave him a wide berth when they met, though Gabby often felt him watching from a distance. What made it worse was that Whiteyes seemed to be collecting followers of his own.

One afternoon Gabby stared gloomily out of the work room window mulling over his ever-present problem. His eyes anchored on the games shed and a plan slithered into his mind causing his hands to stop whittling. With eager anticipation he awaited four o'clock.

The bell hadn't stopped ringing before Gabby was handing in his knife.

In a flash he was outside pulling open the door of the shed. He emerged hugging a soccer ball with which he ran to the center of the field and waited. Other boys jogged toward him and with a mighty kick Gabby sent the ball soaring far to the other end. With a yell everyone took off after it, but Gabby got there first and held them off making motions with his free hand.

"He's dividing us into two teams so we can play a real game." One boy had finally caught on.

"But who'll be coach of the other team?" asked another.

At that moment Whiteyes came trotting across the field and Gabby pointed to him.

The Puerto Rican kid took him up on it. "Hey, you, Whiteyes, Gabby says you got to captain one side for a soccer game."

Gabby watched surprise and suspicion flit across Whiteyes' face. The jerk obviously expected a trick. Gabby nodded, signifying what had been said was true and after another moment's indecision Whiteyes stood to one side with a pleased glint in his eye. The second group previously selected by Gabby seemingly at random, was sent to join Whiteyes and as a soft spring rain began to fall, they lined up against each other.

It started calmly enough and then one kid got an elbow in the ribs and punched his assailant in the nose. From then on, the game became a battle. Gabby had been star of their street game at home until the police stopped it for being too violent. Now he led his team on charges that left the other side frustrated and looking like fools.

Always his own most ferocious tackles were directed at Whiteyes. The ball was soon forgotten as boys wrestled and tumbled on the wet ground and by suppertime everyone was battered, bloody and bruised. Most felt more contented than they had for a long time and another game was planned for next day.

For five days they played during their free time and each game became more savage than the last. Gabby's own fire spread through his team. He thrived on violence and loved the feeling as his fists smashed onto flesh or when he brought someone crashing to the ground. This was what life was all about and he scarcely noticed his own bruises.

At first, he'd wondered why the guards didn't stop them. He'd seen them watch for a while, grin and leave.

Finally, he decided it was like the guard had told him, they couldn't care less what the kids did to each other so long as the men weren't bothered.

While Gabby and his team grew more vicious and eager to play, enthusiasm on the other side waned and Whiteyes could be heard having to urge his team on. Sometimes it sounded more like pleading and Gabby smiled. Only he knew how carefully he had chosen the strongest and toughest for his own. The day he overheard Whiteyes bribe some of his players to come to the field at all he knew his plan had worked. Soon he would have his gang.

THE UNICORN

The sun came and went and although happenings at the school made no intrusion on the life of the Wood, the Unicorn kept watch true to the warning of his dream.

He followed the strange doings of the lodge creatures with interest, especially every afternoon when they tumbled onto the field and battled more roughly than even the most rambunctious lion cubs; then they would all go inside to return and repeat the fight next day. The sounds were so loud that often the Unicorn's delicate ears folded flat against his head to shut them out, and always there were the unpleasant smells. But, fascinated, he could not leave.

CHAPTER VIII

It was Saturday evening and Gabby was bone tired. He'd polished the floor of the staff room and what with moving all the furniture by himself as well as playing a hectic game earlier, all he wanted was sleep. He walked through the semi-darkness to his cubicle and suddenly stopped. The hairs on his neck raised. Someone was in there. He could feel their waiting presence. He always checked the folds of his curtain when he left and when he returned. They had been moved.

Creeping, head poked forward, ears straining for the slightest sound he approached the faintly stirring cloth. He flipped it aside and the figure on the bed sprang to its feet.

Gabby crouched, ready to attack.

"Cool it, Man." Shifty, pale eyes peered through the gloom. "I gotta talk to you private like."

That Whiteyes should invade Gabby's turf was the ultimate sin and by rights he should at least have an ear sliced but Gabby waited, knowing why he was there, his heart already doing a wild dance.

Whiteyes stuttered, scared, knowing he stood on dangerous ground. "Just listen a minute. I can help you. You're slaughtering my guys on the playing field and I admit you're a better fighter than me, but I can talk. We should get together and head up a gang."

The suggestion of a partnership shocked Gabby. The nerve of this idiot saying such a thing to him, and in a boiling rage he flung himself on top of Whiteyes, punching and kicking.

"No, no Gabby. Shut up, you'll have the guards here." The words emerged in smothered grunts. "You're Warlord. You're chief."

Gabby pulled away, allowing his victim to warily unfold.

"Cool down for cris' sake. That's what I meant all along. You'll be Warlord and I'll be your runner and interpreter." Whiteyes' voice wheedled. "We could get good control here with the right kids. About ten of us could run this place. It'd be almost like the streets again. What about it Gabby?"

Gabby's thoughts raced. Maybe it wasn't such a bad idea. He did need a voice, that was for certain, and it would be smart to have Whiteyes where he could keep close watch on him. He was dangerous and some kids seemed to think him important. He'd use him until he decided to talk again, if he ever did.

Gabby had been surprised to find that his inability to speak seemed to freak kids out. Kids didn't know what to expect of someone so different and perhaps full of secrets and hidden powers.

The faint smile that tweaked Gabby's mouth seemed to relax Whiteyes who had been tensely watching him. "What d'ya say?"

Gabby made him wait a few moments more, then nodded.

"Do you want I should call a meeting for tonight?"

Gabby nodded again and flashed twelve fingers, pointing at Whiteyes.

"Midnight at my cubicle. He began to leave but stopped with a worried look. "Who do I get?"

Gabby wished he hadn't asked. He didn't know. He grasped for a solution and on a sudden thought flexed his muscles and pointed to his head.

"The strongest and smartest, right?"

Gabby nodded. At least Whiteyes wasn't stupid. Not all the time anyway. Gabby stood back from the door making it plain he wanted to be left alone and Whiteyes scooted past like a stray dog expecting to have a rock thrown at it.

Gabby, drew a deep breath, carefully straightened the curtain, then smoothed the bed to erase all traces of the interloper. The place his again, he undressed and lay under the covers with his hands behind his head. Tonight, I'll have my gang. His very soul quivered to have his dream so close to reality. I'll keep them scared. Keep them in line all the time. Sure, wish Skull knew. Gabby remembered how ruthless, Skull, Warlord of the Angels had been. No one dared look the wrong way with him around. The whole gang had hated him intensely, but they sure did admire him too. Gabby vowed to make his men feel the same about him. Gabby, Warlord of the ... Yeah, he'd have to think of something good.

Excitement chased away all the weariness of half an hour before and in one quick movement he sat cross-legged on the bed and pulled his drumsticks from their pouch. Excitement poured from Gabby's fingertips as the sticks flew fast, then faster, beating a muffled cadence on the blanket stretched between his knees, carrying him back to remembered streets, far from the alien world that now confined him. He ran again up dark alleys, through secret passageways between tenements, where everything that stirred was familiar; rats, cats or men. The homey smell of garbage, exhaust fumes and cooked fish swirled around him.

A far away clock clashed eleven and sent the remembered world back into the past. Gabby sat stock still. The leadership he had sought all his life was only one hour away. He saw himself leading his gang into battle and figured in time they'd grow in numbers until he was in command of the whole school. Whiteyes would be his voice: And it was a good strong man's growl whereas Gabby's had still been a high kid's treble. Maybe still was. Someday he may try it again but not yet. He envisioned his ferocious little gang, ready to follow his every command, and his chest ached with the glory of it. Time to get ready.

As he slid the sticks back into their sheath, he saw a gleam deep in the leather's blackness. Running his fingers inside he drew out the coiled strand of hair. Strangely pleased to see it again he let it unfold and watched with fascination the sparkles that danced like minute jewels along the ghostly length. Haunting thoughts and emotions brushed him, slipping away before they could be recognized.

I've got to get ready, Gabby thought, why do I sit looking at this dumb thing? He tried to rip the hair in half, but it slid through his hands unbroken. He didn't like the dreamy influence it had on him, and quickly he stuffed it back into his pouch, pushed the drumsticks in on top and jumped off the bed.

He collected a wad of dust from the sill and drew his beard, thicker than before. It looked good in the dark mirror and almost real. He added a smudge more to the upper lip for good measure. He was a Chief, a warlord.

Clang, clang...Midnight. Hurriedly he started to climb into his jeans but slowed down. Better to keep them waiting. Carefully he tucked in his shirt, then ruffled his hair to its utmost height. He winked at his almost invisible image in the mirror. Real cool. Thumbs stuck in his belt loops he swaggered along the hall. It wasn't easy to swagger noiselessly but he managed. At the top of the stairs he paused and looked to the bottom where the guard slept slumped over his desk. Silently Gabby crept up to the third-floor landing and along the corridor to the cubicle almost above his own. His mouth was dry. Taking a deep breath, he flung the curtain aside and stepped through the doorway where he paused, feet apart, hands stiff at his sides, elbows slightly bent like a gun fighter. He knew he looked just like Yul Brynner in that old movie he'd seen five times. Through narrowed eyes he saw faces staring at him through the darkness and, imagining the clink of spurs, he clumped over to the bed and sat solidly in the middle. Actually, his walk to the bed wasn't quite as dramatic as he'd hoped as the floor was packed with bodies he'd had to clamber over but he'd kept his jaw square and his eyes squinted.

Whiteyes shifted nervously beside him and Gabby mouthed something to him twice before he got it. Then the pale kid cleared his throat and spoke in a windy whisper. "Okay, men, who wants to join our gang and rule this new turf? You get one chance." A forest of hands shot up. "That's good otherwise we may have had to show you why you'd made a bad choice. Gabby here is our warlord 'cause he's our only cold-blooded murderer. You all seen about it on TV, right?"

Gabby's insides jumped. He'd killed someone all right, but he never thought about it and he wondered how Whiteyes had recognized him. For an instant he again saw the chair smashing down on his mother's head, shutting off the stream of nagging that was all he ever heard from her.

She'd looked as ugly dead as alive and for a long time he'd waited, expecting her to start yelling at him again. When she didn't all he felt was relief.

"And I'm your second. Right Gabby?"

At least Whiteyes knew the way to do things. Gabby thought as he solemnly nodded.

A shuffle went around the room, the sound of gang status solidifying. These boys were like wolves in their pack, only secure when they had a leader. A gang was the only family most had ever known and now they were beginning to feel safe again.

Whiteyes broke the silence with a whisper. "Now your name and what you was busted for. And keep the noise down, don't want bozo guards crashin' us."

He pointed to a light-haired boy on the far right. "You start."

"Tod's the name. With a hotel rip-off gang. Jewels and cells and rich folk's stuff." Tod nudged the boy next to him.

"Fang, and I can pick anyone's pocket. Best in New York and wouldn't never have been caught 'cept for a rotten squealer."

A hum of sympathy came from the listeners.

A hulking big boy said he was Pirate, in for armed robbery. Then Sims, blackmail and armed robbery both.

And so it went; Tiger, Pete, Josh and Pedro, until eight boys had proudly stated their professions with obvious regret that they had been picked up at what each thought was the highest point of his career. Gabby thought of their talents as his to use. When they got out, with him as leader, they could terrorize a whole city probably.

There was silence as everyone turned toward a figure half hidden in the darkest corner.

"C'mon Beauty, speak up," Whiteyes prodded.

Beauty! What the hell? Gabby wondered how that creep had ever gotten in. He sure wasn't going to have any wimp like that in his gang!

A soft whisper came, "I almost killed a man - with an axe."

Gabby leaned forward. Surprise. Everyone seemed to think murder important. Maybe, even though an "almost," he'd better let the kid stay, for a while anyway.

He shrugged and looked at the others. Not a bad bunch at all barring Beauty and Whiteyes. He'd eliminate them in time. Just looking at Whiteyes made him mad. Suddenly a thought struck him. He tugged a wad of note paper from his hip pocket and started to write with the stub of a chewed pencil. He handed it to his runner and through darkness saw a blush rise in the pallid face.

Whiteyes barely looked up as he muttered. "I'm in for purse snatching and shop-lifting."

A titter ran around the group.

"With assault," he added more strongly, and hurriedly added, "Now what'll we name ourselves?"

This started a frenzy of discussion that had to be quieted with loud hushes. Gabby wasn't about to accept anyone else's idea. He was going to name his own gang himself, It had to be a name that struck fear into the enemy. Something he'd be proud to face Skull with someday. Wasn't murder the crime most looked up to? His own label, murderer, made him Somebody here. He'd never really thought of it much till now but most everyone famous had killed at least one person. Their names were on the TV all the time. His had been for a while. Made him a celeb in his neighborhood for sure. Felt real good. Except he couldn't really enjoy it being locked up right away like he was. Now he could.

He grasped his pencil and wrote two words. Passing the note to Whiteyes he pulled himself straight and tall.

"The Killers," Gabby heard Whiteyes' gravelly voice forgetting to whisper, and wished it was his own. "That's the name Gabby picks. How's about it?"

The boys mouthed and muttered it, sounding tougher with each repetition. Gabby noticed that only Beauty sat quietly hunched in his corner, eyes big and worried.

Testing over, everyone agreed, and The Killers they became.

Now they got down to business and Whiteyes read notes as Gabby wrote them. Tod was given the job of working out a secret sign language and Gabby told them how to make their beds look occupied when they were at the meetings. Then he asked if anyone had heard the T.V. at night.

"I have," Fang whispered. "I didn't know what it was though. I thought it was real."

"I heard it too," said another voice, "Lions and stuff. Had to be T.V. or radio."

"They don't have shows like that on radio."

"They might out here."

"Anyway," Whiteyes interrupted, "Gabby says we got to find out about the T.V. Report before next meeting, then we'll decide what to do about it. 'Snot fair the men should see T.V. and not us."

An angry mutter arose, and someone asked if there'd be food at the meetings and if they'd be every Saturday night.

"I'll get us cake." Beauty spoke for the first time since stating his crime. "I can get that O.K." He offered proudly and Gabby ignored the eyes that sought his for approval.

He wrote a last message. "Meet here every week. Till then, all is one." He'd heard that was said by members of the Crip's whenever they met or parted and now hearing Whiteyes read his message aloud he was elated. Things may not be so bad here after all.

He stood, stalked to the door and left.

Well along the hall he broke into a run, bounding downstairs and into his cubicle. He stood in front of the mirror, shadowy with night, and looked at the image that was himself -- Gabby, Warlord of The Killers. He was a giant. Stronger and more powerful than anyone. He leaned close and looked into that other eye seeing it mean and hard and glittering.

He saw himself running across rooftops carrying a blazing machine gun, his men close behind, and Skull stood way down on the street looking up at him.

A sudden thought sent Gabby scrounging through his belongings until he came up with a black marker. He'd stolen it from the desk in juvenile prison on his way to the bus. Now he carefully drew a teardrop on the inside of his arm. The ink could surely be taken for a real tattoo marking him as a murderer. He remembered a kid he knew bragging how his brother boasted he'd killed someone by wearing a tear drop on his arm. Gabby blew on the ink to be sure it dried without smudging then put three dots on one hand to prove gang allegiance. Someone had told him about that too.

THE UNICORN

Throbbing rhythm had reached through the night and mingled with the beat of the Unicorn's heart. It drew him from the glade in which he had settled and led him to where he looked out at the lodge. Suddenly the building's unrelieved ugliness was dispelled by a brilliant glow which pulsed from a slit in its side. It was the same glimmer which shimmered about the Unicorn's every stride and he watched until it disappeared. Something in there needed him and one day he knew they must meet.

CHAPTER IX

This morning was different from any other in Gabby's life, he awoke being the Warlord he had always dreamed of. Even the sun anointed him with the ray it squeezed through his tiny window and although his heart burst with pride at each "All is one" given by his gang members when they met, he replied with only the most condescending of nods. Today he was omnipotent.

The Killers drifted in groups whenever possible and word spread throughout the school that it was best to give them a wide berth. Strong in their numbers, they beat up boys at the slightest excuse and blatantly snatched things, laughing and jeering at the owner who dare not come after them.

Gabby led them through the halls, proud and complete, urging them on with a glance, knowing that at a snap of his fingers his followers would do whatever he asked.

Spring sunshine grew warm and the afternoon game fizzled. There was no purpose for it now and none of those outside the gang wanted to play against them, so The Killers leaned against the shed and looked tough. Moved on by a guard they broke into smaller groups who tossed the ball or wandered idly. Gabby drifted by himself, glad of the chance to be alone, to think about and savor it all. Besides he wasn't used to having people dog his every step and it got tedious after a while. He passed the kitchen window and looking in saw Beauty peeling potatoes. He stopped, perhaps the boy could sneak him something to eat, he sure felt hungry. But before he could tap on the glass the fat cook came up behind the working boy and stood there with a sweaty hungry look on his face. Then he covered the slender hands with his own and Beauty looked up with a strange, promising smile. Gabby turned away in disgust. Now he knew how Beauty would get cakes and food for the meetings. What matter how he got stuff so long as he did, and he walked away wishing he'd thought to mention that he liked chocolate best.

Since his arrival Gabby had been too preoccupied with problems of getting a gang together to think of much else, but now his thoughts strayed to the surrounding forest they had driven through to get here. Everyone was scared to death of it and the animals Warden said lived there, but today Gabby was afraid of nothing. Besides, with the sun shining so benignly there didn't look much fearsome about the place that he could see. He sauntered toward it and when he looked back the school seemed a long way behind him. He whistled a care-free tune but stayed alert and ready to run, just in case.

He stared into the dim silent depths. It seemed dead. Nothing moved and he was a bit disappointed. Just a boring old place where nothing ever happened at all. Could be ferocious beasts further in of course. Gabby shivered and went back into the sunlight where he wandered aimlessly kicking a pebble in front of him.

Bob-o-link, bob-o-link. The musical yodel vibrated in Gabby's ear causing him to look quickly into the wood on the other side. How different it was over there. Trees formed softer shapes and rustled in a breeze he couldn't feel. Everything seemed alive with color and movement. Gabby went closer and, as the bird called again, he glimpsed it darting from tree to tree. Something about the place excited him and as a breeze tousled his hair, he sniffed sweet smells and felt the birth of a smile somewhere deep inside himself.

He hadn't noticed taking the silver hair from its pouch but now he saw it drifting from his hand, reaching toward the grass like a spider's web, catching colors from the sun and spinning them up and down its length. Entranced, Gabby's thoughts drifted and became soft and floating.

Stupid hair! Anger replaced the weakness he felt reaching inside him, He flung the hair away, but it blew back against his legs. He kicked viciously and trampled it into the ground, but it still rose up and stuck to him.

"Hey, what ya doin'?" Whiteyes ambled across the field, eyes agog with curiosity.

Quickly Gabby snatched the hair and stuffed it into his pocket. No use letting that slob have it. He kicked the pebble back onto the field hoping Whiteyes would think it was all Gabby had been kicking at; but still the nosy punk began to prod among the crumpled ferns muttering, "Did ya find something? What did you see? Weird place this."

Would he never stop? Gabby watched him, hating the whiney voice and the long thick arms. Hating the toes that turned in and the clammy paleness of his skin. Still Whiteyes searched and peered. Gabby wrenched his eyes away and looked into the shades of the wood. His breath caught. A white shape shimmered for an instant and was gone. Maybe I imagined it, he thought, but knew he hadn't and all at once it was imperative that Whiteyes get away from there.

Gabby turned to leave hoping the hated boy would follow, but he didn't. What the hell, Gabby thought and broke into a run, charging through a group of boys and taking their ball which he kicked as hard as he could onto the roof of the building where it hid behind a chimney. He smirked at their concern, knowing they would be punished for losing school equipment. Feeling better, Gabby galloped into the school just as the supper bell rang.

Panting and sweating profusely, Whiteyes joined the line filing into the dining room, He pushed in behind Gabby and gasped, "I saw it, Gabby. How come you weren't scared? It was awful! You won't catch me going near that old wood again!"

Startled, Gabby only just managed to give the shrug the occasion demanded before they separated to their assigned places at the table. What had Whiteyes seen? Was it the white shape? But that wasn't scary. In fact, Gabby remembered feeling distinctly friendly toward it. Whatever it was it had sure scared Whiteyes and that thought was a good one. Whiteyes is an ass, Gabby concluded and turned his attention to the tangle of spaghetti in front of him.

The leader of the Killers felt ten feet tall all week and when time came for the Saturday meeting, he placed himself in the center of Whiteyes' bed and handed his second in command the prepared notes to read.

"Did anyone find the T.V.?" And when no one answered Gabby nudged his runner to ask, "Did you look?"

The faces nodded vigorous assent and one said. "I cased the study and staff-room and there wasn't no T.V. in either for sure."

"I checked out all the staff bedrooms." Gabby recognized Beauty's shy whisper and thought how he might really be quite useful with his run of the place.

No one had found any sign of a television and Gabby figured he'd have to find it himself. It must be somewhere.

"I heard a lion the other night," said Tod.

"Maybe they're all in the forest waiting to attack us!" another voice quavered.

"Maybe monsters like Godzilla."

"A humongous snake almost got me the other day. I won't never go near those trees again." Whiteyes' voice broke and fear shot around the cubicle.

Gabby looked at him in surprise. He'd seen no sign of snakes that day by the wood and he decided Whiteyes probably made the story up or saw a vine and thought it a snake. Dope!

At least it would help keep the others away from what Gabby already thought of as his property, even though he'd only been to the edge that once. Most people were cowards that was for sure, and he looked around him with disgust. What kind of Killers were they-scared by the sound of a T.V. show and Whiteyes lies? With a loud sigh he wrote "I'll find it."

The atmosphere calmed, Whiteyes shuffled papers and read on. "Everyone must prove himself by next week. Show what kind of a badass you are."

A shuffle ran from boy to boy. Relief to get back to their own line of work and have a purpose. Gabby felt good too. He was the gang boss sending his men out on a job. Just by sitting still he could turn the school into a turmoil and who would think to accuse him, the poor dumb kid. He remembered the secret signals and pointed to some papers Tod had rustled throughout the meeting.

"Hey yeah. I got us a whole secret sign language."

Tod eagerly pushed up to the bed and thumped down next to Gabby, thrusting the papers into his hand. He began to explain the black scrawls but before he could get out more than a few words Gabby's fist crashed with a solid punch to the startled boy's ribs. Tod tumbled to the floor where the punch was followed by a kick to his upturned rear.

The room was very still, the only sound that of Gabby's hurried pencil.

"No one sits next to the Warlord without permission. Not ever!" As the cryptic message was read Gabby thought of the time Skull did the same thing to him. Remembered how humiliated and mad he'd been but it had taught him his place. He glowed now with the pleasure of being able to do it to someone else. He did the kicking now. He relayed as how he'd take the code to study first and then they must all memorize it.

"I've got cake." Beauty's whisper collected every thought as all eyes riveted on the paper bag he held.

Each nose sniffed the rich chocolate aroma as the gleaming iced cake was pulled into view and Gabby felt saliva flood his mouth.

"I couldn't get a knife," Beauty whispered. "Cook's awful careful about them."

Gabby quickly grabbed Whiteyes' toothbrush from the dresser, wiped the handle on his shirttail, and handed it to Beauty who began to cut. The boys watched intently.

One piece looked bigger than the rest and it bothered Gabby until Beauty handed it to him, then only the bliss of rich crumbly chocolate existed and when he dropped a piece of icing to the floor Gabby popped it too into his mouth.

As though surfacing from a dream Gabby saw others licking their fingers and signaled the meeting's end. With pleasure he watched them leave, spreading throughout the school to create trouble at his command. When only Whiteyes remained, Gabby wrote his last note of the evening. "What old lady's purse can you snatch?"

Whiteyes muttered, "I'll do O.K. but what about you? Who're you going to kill?"

Gabby grinned and stared knowingly into the colorless face, then he slouched from the room. He had them right where he wanted, he didn't need to prove himself and if he ever did, why, that was no hassle. There wasn't much he couldn't do, that was for certain.

Gabby rested his chin on the narrow window ledge looking through night toward the wood. Could the strange sounds have come from in there? Impossible, reason argued, so many different animals could never live in one place, it must be television. Those piggy bastards downstairs were probably watching it right now.

The wood was different though, even at night it appeared warm and bright while the forest on the other three sides of the school was dark and forbidding. Gabby's eyelids drooped sleepily but suddenly sprang open. A glowing shape, kind of like a horse, had appeared against the trees opposite and now brightened in a pool of moonlight. A halo flickered around it, reminding Gabby of the sparklers sold for Hallowe'en that he used to steal from little kids to swoop through the air and make fancy shapes with. As he watched he knew the creature was aware of him and he scarcely breathed for fear of frightening it away.

And then it was gone, seeming to have taken the moonlight with it. Gabby strained until his eyes hurt but could see nothing and he began to wonder if perhaps he had dreamed the whole thing. He shivered and scooted under the blankets where he squirmed into a tight ball until his breath warmed him. He longed to see if the creature was back but knew if he looked all he would see was black emptiness and somehow, he couldn't bear the disappointment. Even now he was horrified to realize he was almost crying. This was crazy, tough kids like him didn't cry! It had been a vivid dream and that's all.

Abruptly he shot an arm from under the covers, reaching for his clothes on the floor and dragged his jeans into bed with him. A cold button against his chest made him wince but he sighed with relief as he pulled the hair from a pocket. Flinging the jeans aside he dived under the covers again and in his dark cave inspected his possession, watched the familiar sparkling haze - and recognized it.

CHAPTER X

No hiding place was safe. Boys not in Gabby's gang gathered in forlorn groups to angrily bewail thefts of prized belongings. Gabby enjoyed the accusation in their eyes when they looked at him knowing that as Warlord he was cause of their trouble. Everyone knew but the staff and, although things were stolen from them also, they dare not admit it until they found the culprit.

Gabby strutted, seeing himself as one at last with his heroes Crazy Joey, Sonny Pinto and the rest. Someday he'd be as well-known as them too.

It was good the boys lost things. They had too much anyway. Hadn't he seen those big suitcases dwarfing his small bag on the bus? No person needed that much and if they couldn't protect their own property, well, tough luck. Gabby felt his hidden pouch and was content.

One night after a day of spattered showers Gabby was awakened by a laugh that made his skin crawl. He lay still, holding his breath until he feared he would pop.

It came again, strangely eerie, from somewhere outside and he shuddered. A dark shape pushed through his curtain, sending him rigid with fear as it came toward his bed.

"Gabby, hey Gabby, you there?"

Beauty! What the hell was he doing here!

"Did you hear it, Gabby? It's a monster, it must be! Do you think it's coming for us Gabby?"

The small amount of light in the cubicle caught on the fear in the boy's eyes and Gabby's lip curled with scorn.

"What do you think it is, Gabby? I knew you wouldn't be scared. You're the only one who isn't."

Wild eyes locked with Gabby's as the laugh sounded again and this time Gabby felt only curiosity and disdain for the terrified boy beside him. Boldly he swept back his covers, pulled on his jeans and stalked from the cubicle feeling Beauty's admiration follow him all the way down the corridor. Suddenly he remembered that his pouch still lay under his pillow. Damn. He hated to leave it unprotected, but mightn't Beauty misconstrue the reason if he returned? Better keep going, besides, no one would dare steal from him. He'd kill them if they did. Gabby slithered down the staircase and past the sleeping guard at the bottom. He shivered in the draughty passageway that led to the kitchen and wished he wore a shirt. His naked torso felt vulnerable and he tried not to look at the darkest shadows. Warmth closed about him, as he entered the cluttered silence of the kitchen where sinks and counters gleamed dully. Gabby welcomed the jangling pain as he hit his elbow on a corner, rescuing him from his imagination.

The outer door was locked but he soon found the key inside the oven and grinned to think how cook must think it so well hidden.

Gabby knew all those 'safe' places.

In no time he had squeezed past the foul-smelling garbage cans outside and paused to wonder at some newly constructed bench like objects. He couldn't figure them out and moved on into the open. A world full of silence awaited him, black and endless. He stepped back a pace. Perhaps it was better to stay close to the building for a while. He headed toward a lighted window and as he crept a drift of cold wet air chilled him. The nearby sound of men's voices was comforting; he stretched to see over the windowsill. The staff sat drinking coffee and as none faced his way Gabby glanced first around the room to make sure there was no television, then he settled down to listen. He was a confirmed eavesdropper. Everything that wasn't meant to be heard was of intense interest and this time Gabby's attention was fully captured from the first sentence spoken by the math teacher.

"I sure hope that helicopter brings me some mail tomorrow. Outside news will look pretty good."

Gabby pressed closer to the window.

"I'll welcome mail, all right, more supplies, and beer, but I'm not so sure about the new man." The off-duty guard sounded grumpy. "We've got enough on our plates with these blasted kids without a convicted murderer to stir them up."

"Maybe he'll bump a few of them off then he'll save you some work." The speaker laughed.

Gabby couldn't see who it was but recognized the Warden's voice answering.

"No need to worry about Simon. I've met him and he's a ..." The words faded as the speaker turned to the coffee urn and Gabby pressed so hard against the glass it creaked and sent him hastily crouching to the ground. He wanted to hear more but it wasn't worth the risk of getting caught so he leaned against the wall thinking over what he had heard and the more he thought about it the more excited he became.

A real live grown up murderer was coming. A thought threw his feelings into reverse; would the newcomer dim his importance as the only murderer here? What if he tried to take command of the gang?

Now Gabby was tied in knots as apprehension and anticipation tangled.

Shrill laughter rose to a crescendo. It sent a shock from the base of Gabby's spine to the top of his head and for a moment his teeth chattered. He hated it when he let things spook him.

Angrily he pushed away from the wall and strode into the night, ignoring stones beneath his bare feet and the wet wind on his shoulders.

He built upon his anger until he reached the trees and faced them, feet planted wide apart, hands on hips and chin jutting. He dared the laugh to come again.

Nothing happened and his eyes followed moonlit trails that disappeared among silvery edged ferns. Something was wrong. Puzzled Gabby looked back at the way he'd just come. It was dark and unlit with the building barely discernible. Turning again to the wood Gabby's eyes were dazzled by moonlight. How could a moon be in one place and not another? He worried the question but found no solution and squelching any apprehension stepped forward onto the frosty looking grass. It surprised his feet by being warm and soft. Even thicker than the turf he had often disobeyed 'Keep off' signs to cross in the city. He took a few more steps and ferns brushed his ankles while a branch rested against his cheek like a soothing hand. He felt warm and at ease as the edge of dreams came out to touch him.

Abruptly Gabby reached and snapped the branch, stepping back into the field as he dashed the broken end to the ground. Safe from the softness he stood again where there was no moon, no warmth on his shoulders. A place where he could be tough and mean like he had to be to survive. He spat viciously toward the silver wood and his spittle glistened like a diamond where it fell.

"I'll show you. You can't weaken me. I'm Gabby, Warlord of the Killers." Silently he hurled his challenge into the listening wood.

CHAPTER XI

G abby swung around and marched through the brooding darkness, never once looking back. The cold mud of the playing field squidged between his toes and, as he approached the building, he hoped Beauty had told the others where he'd gone. Not one of them would have had the guts. Carefully, he locked the door of the kitchen behind him, replaced the key in the stove and, whistling between his teeth, reached the stairs. He stopped.

There was no light and the guard was gone. Probably sneaked off to bed, Gabby decided and bounded upward to be blinded by the beam of a flashlight.

He spun around to escape but fingers held his arm with such force he could do nothing but wait for the pain to stop.

Fuckit. Fuckit, Fuckit, he thought.

"So, you're the thief. Creepin' around swipin' stuff from everybody. I hope Warden gives you what you deserve."

The guard's voice was a low growl and his breath smelled of whiskey. He released Gabby's arm and shoved a cold flashlight against his ribs. "Get on down, Warden will be pleased about this."

Gabby sauntered as coolly as if he was going to the corner store for a Coke. He felt eyes watching from above and was glad of this chance to show how invulnerable he was to anything this place could throw at him.

As he entered the room he had spied into not long before, the men turned toward him, and he sank into the cocoon of impassibility he wore during all encounters with adults. Through half shut eyes he saw them lower coffee cups to peer at him. Warden took a long sip as he walked toward him, examining Gabby over the rim. Without looking at the guard he asked, "What's the problem here?"

Puffed proud the guard stepped forward. "I caught this kid sneaking upstairs. I reckon he's the thief we been looking for." He pushed Gabby. "Get into the light, boy, so Warden can see you."

Knocked off balance Gabby lost his careful pose and shot a look of hatred toward the guard. He noticed sweat shining through the stubble on his head and along the flattened nose and wondered if the man had ever been a fighter.

"Face front, boy."

Gabby turned forward.

"What's your name, boy? "The warden seemed to be speaking from a great height.

Gabby couldn't believe the man didn't know who he was. Him, the most important kid in the whole school.

"Come on now, it's too late to play games."

Gabby wished he had his shirt on, muscles look bigger when they're hidden. He lifted his chin a notch staring at the air over the warden's head and wished he had his gum to chew.

"Boy, you'd better speak up or you'll be getting more than you bargained for."

From the corner of his eye Gabby saw the woodworking teacher come toward them. "That's Arthur."

Gabby's stomach curled and his lip twitched.

"Of course, I should have known. Why didn't you speak sooner?" Warden was mad and his voice got louder and louder. "What's the kid like?"

"Tough, smart when he wants to be." The teacher thought for a moment. "I suspect he's leader of that little gang that's started up. What you say you brought him in for?"

"Stealin" the guard spoke authoritatively.

"What did he take?" Warden asked.

"Well he didn't actually have nothin' on him. Probably hid it somewhere."

The teacher shook his head. "I'm surprised. Wouldn't think he'd steal. He'd get someone to do it for him or fight for what he wanted. He's a scrapper. Break someone's arm, maybe, or even his neck but not this sneaky kind of stealing. Does he admit it?"

The guard looked disgusted. "Jeez, you just said yourself he can't talk."

"He can nod, can't he?"

Gabby felt the warden watching him as the two men wrangled and now the man raised a hand to silence them. "All right let's see what I can get out of him. Arthur, did you steal anything? Nod yes or no."

At sound of the hated name Gabby closed up tight. Not one hint of an answer would they get, not if they beat him to death for it. He wondered if anyone listened outside the door and hoped they did. He'd show them. Staring until the room was a blur, he ran through all the dirty names he could think of. He hated the smell of coffee on the man's breath and tried not to inhale until he really had to.

"Come on, Arthur. I'll believe you. Just nod one way or the other whether you were stealing or not. If you admit it I'll let you off light."

Gabby forced his head to stay still, slitted his eyes and worked the muscle in his cheek like they did in movies. He was Che Guevara. He was tougher than tough. He was badass through and through.

"Damn it, kid, I'll have you beaten in a minute if you don't show some cooperation!"

Gabby could see the man's hands twitch like claws, but they were the only thing that moved in the room. He wished something would happen to break this stalemate because his nose itched, and his head wanted to bob and turn. More than anything he wanted to go to bed.

"Damn kids!" The warden's explosion released them all.

"Give him six of the best."

It crossed Gabby's mind to be grateful now that he had left his drumsticks upstairs. He must get that hiding place ready...Whack ... the lash burned across his back.

He felt everyone in the room watching, the leather stung again and again but Gabby thought about other things and barely noticed the blows. His eyes roamed the books on the shelf in front of him. "Crime and Punishment." That's a laugh, all my real crimes have never been punished and my punishments were all for things I never did.

Killing Ma wasn't a crime. That had just been the natural course of things.

Beating over he straightened and stretched even though it hurt like hell. Face arranged in the same bored expression he turned toward the watchers, yawned, and left the room.

Next morning, apart from moving carefully, he showed no sign of last night's beating, but the boys knew and glanced at him with admiration. In breakfast lineup Beauty whispered, "I'm sorry they caught you, Gabby. Did you find out what it was?"

For a second Gabby was puzzled, then he remembered the eerie laughter and gave Beauty a negative shake of his of his head.

"I worried about you. Here."

The line moved on and Gabby felt something thrust into his hand. When he sat at table, he saw it was a tube of ointment. I don't need junk like that, he thought, and stuffed it into his pocket. But somehow, he couldn't feel as indifferent as he wanted, it was the only gift he had ever received apart from the drumsticks, and he felt it now and again throughout the meal.

Later he pried up the loose board under his bed to display the cavity he had prepared in case of need. That need was now –his back was way too painful to bear his drumstick's sling across it, but his most valuable possessions would be safe here. He recovered them from under his pillow and, as an afterthought, put the tube of ointment in beside them. It would be a waste to use his only other present.

The boys looked at him with new respect but what Gabby enjoyed even more was Whiteyes' envy. As Runner, the boy was liable to assume more importance than he should. Gabby knew he must keep that in check.

During the first lesson his eyes roamed to the window and suddenly he remembered the helicopter. How could he have forgotten? Bringing a murderer too! Gabby sat bolt upright; his full attention concentrated on the cloudless sky.

It took forever until lunchtime arrived but at last, he sat eating tapioca, separating each rubbery marble in his mouth, feeling its smoothness with his tongue before he bit it in half and pulled the next from his cheek. His mouth was still half full when Warden tapped a water glass for silence.

"Boys, go to your cubicles now and stay there until the bell rings for class to start again. No visiting. No noise. Understood?" A sharp glance around the room and he left.

A tingle zoomed from Gabby's stomach, across his shoulders; it must be almost time! He plunged through the boys who jostled toward the door. "Hey, Gabby, what's up?" Tod shouted.

Gabby didn't want to stop but couldn't resist displaying his knowledge so, producing pad and pencil, he scrawled, "Helicopter" and held it high for all to see. Then he sprinted up to his cubicle where he leapt onto his bed and pushed his face against the window, scanning the sky. It seemed extremely empty. Gabby searched for the faintest speck until his head ached and he sat down.

Immediately he thought he heard an engine but when he looked there was nothing. Perhaps if he if he stopped thinking about it... He pulled the secret code from under his mattress to study but always helicopters and scarred faces swam between his eyes and the paper. He recovered his drumsticks and vigorously beat his pillow until the sound seemed to rock the building. That can't all be me! Realization shot him to the window and, enveloped by the throbbing roar, he watched whirring blades cut the sunlight as they lowered an insect-like body onto the playing field. Staff members ran toward it, clothes whipping wildly until the blades slowed and stopped- leaving an exhausted silence. Gabby held his breath as he watched the door in the machine's side open.

THE UNICORN

The Unicorn galloped away from the clearing, terrified by the roaring bird that had caused a gale among the trees. He fled until there were no sounds but those of the wood and then he stopped. Gradually the peace of long unvisited surroundings soothed his trembling. It was good to be back; to leave the tension of past months. Surely the shiny bird was the signal ending his responsibility. The Unicorn's heart leaped with lightness as he crossed beloved glades and trails he had known for all time. He knew when a vixen tumbled her cubs beside her earth not three feet from where he silently passed, and he paused to admire the colors of a Macaw as it worked its way up a branch, beak over claw, beak over claw. It winked at him and he move on. A cougar crossed his path, bounding high and pouncing on shadows.

In a shining second, they were gone and the wood was quiet but for the ripple of running water. Usually the Unicorn would break into a trot and jump the wide stream which sang and chuckled before him but today he felt too relaxed and as his feet touched the edge an alligator rose to make a bridge. A few careful steps and the Unicorn reached the other bank, giving a soft snort of thanks as the reptile submerged.

In a clearing of Pongola grass the Unicorn sank down and rolled. The grass tangled into a mat massaging his sleek hide, and finally he polished his horn, running it through and through the plaited blades.

CHAPTER XII

Catching a glare of light the helicopter door swung open and two men in fawn overalls jumped to the ground. Gabby quickly deserted them for the figure in white who hesitated in the doorway above. The murderer! He tried to see details, but the man was too far away and Gabby had to give up and watch the others unload boxes and cartons until they formed a jagged mountain.

The two men paused for a breather and leaned against their cargo as they scrutinized the building. "Place looks a bit beat around the ears already, don't it Tony."

The voices floated clearly to Gabby.

"Not bad considering, I guess," Tony stretched. "That railing you carved still looks pretty good, Joe. We'll be able to see how our work holds up if we keep this job every month. C'mon let's unload the livestock."

At that the third man, who had stayed inside, began to push out large wooden boxes. He handled them carefully as though they held something valuable. Gabby watched, eaten with curiosity, until six crates sat in a neat row on the ground and there they were left as the men came inside.

Gabby turned away from his cubicle's slit of a window and rubbed his cheek where it was numb from pressing against the bars. Whatever else was out there he sure hoped some gum was included. But why had they acted as though those crates held something breakable? Nothing valuable would be sent here.

Voices returned him to his watch post and he saw the two men climb into the helicopter, start the engine, and, with a great whirring, lift slowly into the air, leaving a small group from the school bent against the wind like storm-tossed crows. The machine swung in a circle and then wheeled away over the wood until it was no bigger than the swallows that swooped around the building. Then it was gone.

The sky looked awful empty and lonely.

The sound of the bell jerked Gabby back from space and he joined the others in the stampede downstairs. The chatter was deafening as those who had been able to see told those who hadn't what had happened.

The guard called out several names, including Gabby's, and ordered them outside to move the supplies. Gabby scowled and kicked the ground but inwardly was overjoyed to be chosen and his eyes searched eagerly for the figure in white. There he was by the distant crates; a real cold-blooded murderer. As he crossed the space between them Gabby imagined the cruel vicious face and pondered whether to be aggressive or offhand at this first meeting. He hadn't made up his mind when he found himself looking into the bearded face of an old man whose vivid blue eyes smiled as he said, "Careful now, lad, they're all upset from the flight."

Gabby's breath flew right out of him. Was this the murderer? This crummy old man with not one scar to be seen?

Disappointment flooded him and then a tinge of relief as he thought that at least there would be no leadership threat...then again, maybe the old man was just a good actor and was really tough underneath. Maybe he hid his meanness to keep everyone off guard. So many thoughts whirled through Gabby's head he hardly noticed taking the box held out to him.

"There, there little lady, you'll soon feel at home."

Gabby peered to see who the old man talked to in the crate with such a lopsided feel to it. By leaning forward he could see through the wire netting which covered the front and there sat a fat white rabbit, twitching her whiskers as she looked at him with worried red eyes. Gabby almost dropped the box in surprise. He'd never seen a live rabbit before.

"That's Ellie, and I'm Simon by the way."

The voice was soft and rumbly, and when Gabby looked up, he noticed that Simon's nose twitched like the rabbits.

"Know anything about these critters? No? Well you'll soon learn. Take her around the corner by the kitchen. They've got a place ready there."

Gabby put on the stubborn look he always wore when asked to do something, but the man seemed not to notice and turned to another box, speaking softly into it.

The crate was growing heavier by the moment, so Gabby took it to one of the shelves he had wondered about the night before. Once settled, he leaned close to the netting and inspected the rabbit who was doing the same to him. The only rabbits Gabby had seen, except in pictures, were made of chocolate. In fact, the only animals he had known were rats, stray cats and the blind old collie that belonged to the corner newsman. He had never touched one.

With two heavy hops the rabbit rested its pink nose on the wire, flopping its ears back on furry shoulders. Gabby picked some grass from a tussock by the wall and poked them at the nervously chomping teeth which squiggled the green blades out of sight. Gabby grinned and rubbed his finger against the soft forehead which pushed back at him.

"Cute, aren't they?" A kid wearing glasses had come around the corner and now set down another cage.

Gabby roughly shoved Ellie's face and turned away with a contemptuous shrug hoping the boy hadn't seen him pet the creature. He started back to the field and the boy trotted alongside, wheezing asthmatically. "I like rabbits."

Gabby walked faster.

"My dad gave me two once and they had babies. Then a cat killed them all and dad said I couldn't have anymore. I sure felt bad and when I get out of here, I'm goin' to have me a whole farm full of them!" The eyes looked belligerently through their wire frames, daring Gabby to deny his dream.

Gabby just snorted and thought how dumb some kids were. They never learned that you couldn't let yourself like things. Not if you wanted to be Someone. It was the difference between him and the rest; what made him Warlord and them just followers. He'd learned by the time he could walk that if you didn't care whether your mother was nearby it made no difference that she hardly ever was. After that, with a few reminders, he just grew tougher. "Himself" was all that mattered, all he needed.

Simon waited with two more cages.

"What did you bring rabbits here for?" the boy asked.

"Why for food," Simon replied and Gabby felt a bit of a shock.

"Not these ones of course, but their babies. We've got to try to be self-supporting in case the helicopter can't make it sometime." He carefully set a crate in each boy's arms. "Now you get these put down back there and then, seeing as there's only two left, you," he looked at Gabby, "Come back to me and you..." With a wave of walnut skinned hands Simon released the smaller kid, "Can see if the others need help"

At first Gabby was glad to be chosen over the other boy, especially when he saw disappointment on his pudgy face, but then he started to wonder what motive the man had for keeping him. Probably thinks 'cause I'm bigger I can work harder, Ha! The old bastard has another think coming if he expects me to be his slave.

When he returned alone, he found Simon struggling to lift a cage larger than the others and Gabby watched until the old man was finally upright with it safe in his arms. "Whew!" He gasped. "He's a heavy one." A thump came from inside. "This is Buck. He's kind of mad about this whole thing. Never mind, old fellow, you'll soon see your wives again. You pick up Daisy and let's go."

This last was to Gabby and in a short time they stood looking at the row of six cages.

"They tell me your name's Arthur and you can't talk," Simon said. "Well, the rabbits don't talk either and we get along just fine, besides I say enough for two people."

Gabby watched the rabbits' wriggly noses.

"You know something else? You don't look one bit like an Arthur. Not at all. What do you want me to call you?"

Gabby glanced at him. Maybe the old guy wasn't so bad. Then maybe he was just trying to make a good impression. Whatever… Gabby took out his pad and pencil and wrote his name.

"Gabby. That's much better. Shows you've got a sense of humor. Now, let's get these rabbits fed and watered, they've had a pretty nerve-wracking day of it. Here, you fill these little bottles with water and hang 'em upside down on the netting so the critters can drink whenever they want. While you do that, I'll get a sack of feed."

He disappeared and Gabby sat right down on the ground where he was, his automatic reaction to any order. The rabbits scratched at their doors and a cold wind sent dust swirling. Gabby stood up. He might as well find out how the gadgets worked. He filled the first two at the spigot and hung them by their twist of wire.

Ellie was first to try hers. She pushed her split lip up to the glass stem and drank in fast gulps. Gabby watched bubbles rise through the water, watched her eyes glow red in a patch of sun. Then she scratched behind one ear and her hind foot moved so fast it was only a blur.

Thump. Thump.

Cool!

Buck wanted some. He was a tough old devil he was, and Gabby filled another bottle. Soon each rabbit had its water container hanging like a gleaming icicle.

Simon struggled around the corner carrying a heavy sack, and Gabby watched him take it to the nearby storage room and wrestle it into a corner.

A lot stronger than he looks, Gabby thought, inspecting him, and wondered where he hid his viciousness. Perhaps he just goes nuts now and again. Maybe at full moon. His face sure had a lot of lines and there could easily be a scar hidden under that grizzled beard. It wasn't an ugly face, Gabby admitted to himself, the lines weren't scowly like some people's and the eyes were clear, as if someone else was hidden inside. Someone young, used to looking out across distances.

"Well, Gabby, seeing as they won't let either of us carry a knife what can you come up with to cut this sack?"

After a second's thought Gabby went to the garbage cans where he rummaged around and came back with a sharp tin lid. He handed it over.

"Well done, lad. Why don't you just cut the string here, then it should pull undone. Good."

They fed the rabbits and covered the cage floors with shavings. At first Gabby did a minimum of work, but when Simon just whistled and worked along it seemed easier to move to the same rhythm. When they finished Simon checked over each rabbit and the way he talked so soothingly, and rubbed the backs of their necks, seemed strange to Gabby so he wished he didn't have to listen.

"They seem none the worse for their journey and I guess that's all we can do for now. Thanks a lot Gabby, you're a good helper. Would you like to have this as a steady job? They said I could have a boy once a day with cage cleaning and tomorrow I want to build a run for them. I'd as soon have you if you're willing. The rabbits like you."

Gabby looked at the contentedly munching bundles of fluff. It sure beats washing floors, he told himself, and nodded in agreement.

"Good," Simon looked pleased. "I'd better get inside and see what Warden has lined up for me. S'long, Gabby."

Gabby stood alone in the spring sunshine hearing the rabbits rustle beside him. Strange old guy seems to like me. Nobody ever likes me. Must have a gimmick.

Slowly Gabby wandered back into the school, his sore back reminding him of last night. So much had happened since then he'd almost forgotten about it. He slipped into the last half hour of woodworking and instead of the soap dish his instructor thought he made Gabby carefully carved a trough for Buck.

THE UNICORN

The Unicorn awoke in the milk-like mist of dawn and sleepily stretched each leg, then his neck, arched high and tight. He grazed, his spirit as calm as the trailing threads of night. A hummingbird chastised him politely as he bounced her nest in passing and zipped around him once like a tiny flame. A lark flung its song to the brightening sky and somewhere a kookaburra gave a comradely chuckle.

The Unicorn wandered dreamily from clover to leaf, from glen to glade.

Caw! Caw! A raucous cry from the tree above startled him and a chill crept into his heart. Ahead the ugly shape of the school squatted smugly under the noonday sun. The unicorn's wide nostrils breathed in the scent of rabbits. Trapped rabbits in need of rescue. But he didn't know how without endangering the secrets of the Wood.

CHAPTER XIII

An unfamiliar feeling filtered into Gabby's dedication to being seen as the most dangerous and vicious leader of the Killers: the one whom everyone feared as he had once feared and envied the warlord who ruled his own city neighborhood.

That afternoon after he met Simon something burned like a small ember throughout the remainder of the day and not until he lay in bed at night did he seek it out and try to identify it. Evasive as a puff of smoke it escaped until he recognized it as anticipation for morning. Then came doubt. Doubt that as Warlord of The Killers he should have accepted the job of looking after rabbits. Doubt that he should so willingly do Simon's bidding. Hadn't he almost volunteered for the job? He'd never volunteered to do anything in his whole life! How could the gang respect a leader who looked after fuzzy, cute rabbits? You had to be toughest of the tough to be war lord.

A mosquito zoomed past and he felt the slight tickle as it landed on his arm. Smack. Only a dot of blood remained and he wondered whose.

With morning a small anxious feeling awoke inside Gabby and as soon as he got downstairs it sent him to the bulletin board. The old duties opposite his name were crossed out and instead was the one word "Rabbits."

Stifling a charge of relief, he gave a fine display of disgust, earning the gang's commiseration, and then tried not to look forward to his new chore.

The order to assemble at the far end of the playing field after lunch surprised everyone but, welcoming any change in routine, the boys shouted and banged into each other on their way to where Simon stood surrounded by forks, shovels, hoes and balls of string. The noisy crowd stopped their horseplay out of curiosity not knowing what to expect of this newcomer who was neither one of them nor staff.

They watched him pick up a packet. "Well boys, this here's some seeds and instead of a picture of lettuce on the front here I want us to have the real McCoy growing in the ground. Now I can only use ten of you, so I'll divide you right down here and the rest go back to class."

Gabby was relieved to be in the group that stayed.

"Now if you'll each take a fork, we'll dig a square from that dandelion over there to where I drove in the stakes. We're a bit late for planting but with luck we'll get a crop."

Gabby saw Whiteyes straggling away with those who left and was glad to be rid of him. He got a fork and listened as Simon told them what to do.

The old man's trying to con you into working again, something whispered in Gabby's head and he became confused and angry and begrudged each bit of effort that pushed the fork into the ground. He'd never used one before but when Simon offered help, he made it plain he didn't need any and turned his back. Simon just smiled and moved on.

The turned soil smelled rich and the row Gabby finished looked good. He stabbed a worm that wriggled through the crumbly soil and watched the two halves squirm. When another surfaced, he just covered it over and then cussed himself and looked around to make sure no one had seen.

When all the defined area resembled a turbulent sea the boys flung down their tools and complained over their blistered palms.

"Now we'll rake it smooth so we can plant." Simon already worked on a corner.

The boys glared rebelliously and one growled. "Shit, if I'd wanted to be a gardener, I'd a bin one. You take your rakes, old man, and ..."

"Work!" The watching guard's order cracked like a whip, and the grumbling boys took up rakes and began to scrape them across the soil. The rhythm soothed them into quiet and sweet earth smells rose to Gabby's nostrils. He drifted into lethargy, eyes automatically following the rake back and forth.

"Well done, Gabby." Simon's gentle praise snapped him back to awareness and he saw the smooth patch he had made. For an instant pleasure touched him, then he saw the smirk on the face of the boy next to him and in one quick ragged stroke he dragged the rake through his work, leaving it scarred and defaced.

He turned to see what effect his action had on Simon but the old man had turned away and now sorted packages.

"Ha! Look what Gabby did!" A boy chortled and prepared to follow his example but a blow across the side of his head from the guard sent him back to work. Gabby spat and leaned on his rake.

By late afternoon they were finished, and slightly wiggly rows ended in stakes displaying package-pictures of carrots, beets, beans and all the other vegetables Simon had brought.

"Thank you, boys. You did a fine job." Simon straightened the final stake and stood up; the white smock he always wore as clean as when he had started although he had worked as hard as anyone.

The boys stood for a moment looking over what they had done. The results were impressive, and it seemed as if however hard they tried they could find nothing derogatory to say. Gabby walked with them toward the school, half hoping for Simon's call, and when it came it was all he could do to stop from spinning around and running back to him.

"Gabby, lad, I guess it's time for you and me to get to our rabbits. Could you help tote some tools?"

Throwing a look of disgust toward the other boys he turned slowly and, hands in pockets, strolled back to where Simon was already loaded with rakes and forks and bags.

Face twisted with annoyance Gabby picked up what was left and noticed Whiteyes and then some others around the school door looking out at him and laughing to see him loaded like a pack mule. He'd pay them back for that, especially that slob Whiteyes.

He was just about to drop his load not caring what trouble it got him into when he noticed that Simon walked with a strange limp. Gabby began to mimic it, getting more outrageously exaggerated at each step. Boys lined up to watch, nudging each other and laughing, cheering Gabby on as he flung one leg stiffly to the side, arms flailing, head bobbing, eyes crossed. Applause followed as he hopped and cavorted out of sight around the corner of the building. Unexpectedly Simon stopped, turned to Gabby, and winked. Then he walked on with no trace of any limp at all.

Gabby stood astonished. It looked as though the old guy had done it on purpose. But why? Surely not to get him out of a spot. Gabby didn't want to believe that, but he had to admit Simon had guts and was getting pretty hard to dislike even though Gabby tried his hardest. He felt a pain in his stomach, that's what the trouble was, indigestion, it could muddle the mind sometimes. He stopped worrying and jogged to catch up, grasping his awkward load tightly, until they walked side by side and the rabbits wobbled their noses in greeting.

As days passed the time Gabby spent with Simon and the rabbits separated itself from the rest of his life. Like being asleep, those hours were his own private time, but never, even to his deepest soul, would he admit how much he depended on them and enjoyed being in that out of the way corner. If he stroked a soft head sometimes, he was careful not to let Simon see and when asked to do something he never forgot to look annoyed. Not that Simon seemed to notice, he just went on as though Gabby were the most willing companion he could wish for.

Back with the boys Gabby was as savage and demanding a warlord as ever ruled a gang. Ruthlessly he drove them to harass and steal from everyone in the building, and the more they achieved the prouder and more powerful he felt. It wasn't what they stole but the feeling he got of being looked up to, almost worshipped, as the boys squirmed like happy spaniels at his least sign of praise.

After the helicopter's next arrival pickings were exceptionally good as many boys received packages from home, the best from which was soon proudly displayed at The Killer's weekly meeting. Gabby ridiculed those who received gifts, calling the parcels conscience sops, and he laughed at the misery when they were stolen.

Beauty presented a cake at each meeting and his eyes gleamed to see it devoured so speedily it almost might never have been.

Now that everyone knew the secret sign language, Gabby didn't have to depend on Whiteyes so much and he began to plot ways of getting rid of him altogether.

The new language had taken a while to learn and some had to be changed, like scratching the chin to let it be known cook was out of the kitchen in case anyone wanted to steal food. Unfortunately, quite a few boys continuously scratched pimples causing more than one unexpected confrontation with cook.

One day, while making a detour to make sure the rabbits had water, Gabby discovered the first sprouts in the garden and bent low seeking more. It became a habit to come first thing each morning and he began to notice things like early dew clinging to minute spears and once put a droplet onto the tip of his finger to taste but it was gone before his tongue felt it. He even began to water the vegetables without having to be asked.

The sixth meeting was a good one. The gang munched stolen chocolate bars and boasted of their exploits.

"Look at this!" A watch swung from Fang's grubby hand. "I nabbed it right out of the fat guard's pocket. Ho, won't he be mad! Wish I could see it. He thinks he's so bloody smart, the way he swaggers around. He'd give his eye teeth to find which of us done it. 'Fraid to haul you in again Gabby without proof but he'd sure like to."

Gabby shrugged. He didn't care about any guards so long as they didn't hassle him. He despised them, too lazy to even do an all-out search for the stolen stuff and, of course, none of the kids ever reported when things were swiped from them.

"Reckon the men hate it here as much as we do?" Pedro asked.

"Hell no," Tod spoke as one who knows, "They get booze, free living and good pay with a chance to go home after six months. They got it made while we rot."

"Look what I got."

Everyone peered at the object in Tiger's hand.

"Hey, that's a radio!"

"Wow, let's hear it!"

"It's got no batteries," said Tiger.

"Ah shit. what good's it then?"

"What d'ya mean? It's a good radio." Tiger sounded angry. "I mean it almost works, don't it? Everything else is good and anyway, maybe someday I'll find batteries."

There seemed an aura of hope to the silent black plastic and each boy touched it before Pedro pulled out a fancy tie, recognized as the one proudly flaunted by the biggest braggart in school. Whispered cheers greeted it and so the meeting went and when they broke up no one remembered that Beauty had not produced his usual cake.

No one but Gabby. He noticed. Who the hell did the faggot think he was? Sluffing off while everyone else worked. Gabby galloped upstairs, welcoming the excuse to beat up the kid whose gentle ways annoyed him more every day. He elbowed the cubicle curtain aside and faced Beauty who hunched under covers, staring with terrified rabbit eyes.

When he recognized Gabby fear fled and quickly he began to speak. "I'm glad it's you, Gabby. I wanted to talk to you. I know you're mad because I didn't bring a cake but I couldn't!"

Gabby saw a pleading rabbit head flatten as the tremulous whisper continued. "You don't know what it's like, Gabby. I hate it and I won't do it anymore. When you're small and look like I do in the place where I lived it's the only way to survive." The whisper

78

was defiant for a moment and then dropped back to beseeching misery. "I can't stand it anymore, Gabby, say I don't have to."

The voice beat through darkness like moth wings, fluttering around Gabby's ears, beating back his anger, and for a moment he imagined Beauty's heart hammering light and quick like that of the rabbit Simon had given him to hold that afternoon. The anger and impatience he wanted wouldn't stay.

"I'll steal, Gabby. I tried once before, but I wasn't any good. I'm older now, maybe I'll be better. Please don't kick me out of the gang. I want to be tough like you. Let me try."

Gabby left. He was glad he couldn't speak. After all, why should he care what the kid did so long as he pulled his weight somehow. They didn't need cake anyway.

Back in his own cubicle however his mood changed. He'd been a fool. He should have thrashed the kid. Taught him a lesson like he'd intended. Whatever had come over him? Gabby grabbed his pillow and began to punch it. He hammered furiously until his arms ached, half hoping a guard would hear and come to arrest him and take him away for another beating.

CHAPTER XIV

Beginnings of summer pushed back the morning chill and for the first time the boys did their calisthenics without shivering. Wood smoke drifted lazily upward from the kitchen chimney and there was a lot of gazing from windows during lesson time. Boys minds drifted and they longed for the freedom hinted at by mellow winds.

The helicopter had come and gone for the third time which meant fresh vegetables, fruit and meat for a few days before they returned to canned and dried foods. Gabby whittled a piece of wood longing for the hour when he could escape to Simon and the rabbits.

He had stopped acting tough in that separate world they shared. Simon never seemed to notice, so it wasn't worth the trouble. Sometimes Gabby just sat in the sun watching the old man snuggle the soft bodies to his grizzled cheek and listening to his gentle crooning. It was like being in a bubble where Gabby could relax and become the fourteen year old he was. He let himself hold the rabbits and scratch their necks, and once when Simon wasn't around, he rested Ellie against his cheek where she snuggled softly and tickled him with her whiskers.

While he cleaned their cages, they hopped around his feet and one afternoon he proudly showed Simon how Daisy came to him when he clicked his tongue and offered a pellet of food.

"They sure like you, Gabby." Simon's eyes smiled as he spent minutes watching as though he had nothing more important to do in the whole world.

Gabby didn't see him as old anymore and didn't even feel annoyed when asked to do something. He admitted to himself that Simon wasn't so bad and silenced the warning that jarred through him. This was different. And Simon was like no one he had ever met.

The Killers lived in awe and terror of their leader and only Beauty dared enter Gabby's cubicle. He left hidden gifts to prove he was working like he had promised, stealing successfully, and Gabby made no complaint. Now the pouch was safe around his chest while the secret compartment in his floor held, as well as the tube of ointment, a penknife, odd pieces of candy, some strong-smelling hair oil and a silk scarf. Gabby gloated over his acquisitions but never acknowledged them, never nodded a thank-you. Still the gifts kept coming.

"Shh," Simon bent over a cage and Gabby slowed his precipitous arrival to tiptoe and peer over the smocked shoulder. He saw a mass of mouse-like creatures squirming against Ellie's soft underbody. Following his first excitement, disappointment set in. They weren't at all the miniature rabbits Gabby had expected. He wondered if maybe something was wrong with them.

Simon read his thoughts. "Pretty ugly, aren't they? Won't be long though 'til they're the cutest things on God's earth. I'll bet you and I didn't look too beautiful at their age, eh?"

Gabby grinned and felt better about it. He'd never seen anything so young and he watched, fascinated.

"We'd better leave her be, she's a bit nervous."

They fed the other rabbits and suddenly a large splash of rain fell and then another, battering ever more quickly on the cage roofs. The air had a singed smell to it and dust rose in small volcanoes where the drops pierced the ground. Man and boy ran to the shelter of the overhang next the kitchen and hunkered down against the wall. Black clouds swirled overhead blotting the blue of only moments before and light drained away.

Simon carefully lifted the edges of his smock over his knees away from the dirt and brushed them off. He saw Gabby watching and answered the question in his eyes. "I like to wear a smock when I work with animals. Figure it makes them comfortable to see me always look the same. Smell the same too."

Thunder rolled somewhere behind the black pines.

"Familiarity is important to creatures, you know." Simon's voice grew soft as he looked back into a memory. "I once had a sow with a brood of piglets. She'd never seen me out of my work clothes till one day my wife made me get all dressed up to go to a wedding. Well, just as we were about to leave, I thought I'd check on old Patch. She took one look at me in those fancy duds and turned right around and ate three of her piglets. I guess she'd have et the lot if I hadn't left fast!"

Gabby looked to see if he was kidding but it didn't seem so. He sure hoped Ellie wouldn't eat her babies next time he looked at her. Simon's thoughts were far away, and the rain pelted down harder, shutting the two of them into a private world.

Staring into space Simon began to speak in an easy, remembering kind of way. "Animals are important to me. I guess they're the reason I never took up smoking. I had a big old hound when I was a kid who went everywhere with me and one day after school a bunch of us got behind the bike shed and smoked a pack of cigarettes. Well, old Red just curled up his nose and slunk off home. When I got back, he wouldn't have a thing to do with me until I got rid of that cigarette smell. I guess I paid more heed to his opinion than anyone else's 'cause I never smoked again. Smart dog, saved me a lot of money over the years." The voice drifted off into the rain and Gabby waited, hoping for more.

He couldn't remember anyone ever really talking to him before. Not like this, showing the inside of his mind.

Gabby thought back over Simon's words, imagining a world he had never seen, with dogs and pigs and a home. He hungered for more and shuffled hopefully. A bluster of rain blew in at them.

Simon lifted his face to the wetness. "We had rains like this back home. I remember it pounding on the roof of the dairy at milking time and me and the cows all safe and warm from it. Have you ever been in a barn full of cows, Gabby? It does a soul good. Soft breathing, they are and peaceful. The peace seems so thick it makes you think how silly it is to get all het up about the goings on in the world. But you're a city boy, aren't you? I figure every kid should be sent to spend some time in a barn full of cows. Not these newfangled kinds of things where the cows walk in whenever they want to and are milked and fed by machine. No, not them but where the cows all stand in their own stanchions, with their own names hanging over their heads, eating feed the man gives them; the man who sits, head pressed against warm gurgling flank, sending white streams of milk into foam that rises in the bucket between his knees. Oh Gabby, they're taking away the goodness of the world with their machines."

In the silence Gabby felt sadness for things lost. Things he had never known existed. He had never imagined there could be anything different to his own streets.

"I had a fine farm once, Gabby. My dad started it and finally we had the whole valley growing like the Garden of Eden right there. Sure it got cold in winter and I got tired enough to drop at times but they were good honest feelings and you could trust everything. 'Cept maybe old Honor; the bull, but even him you could trust to be ornery. Sometimes I'd walk up onto the hill and look down on it all, thinking of my family there in the house and everything as far as I could see enclosed in the hills so safe and good. I like to burst from happiness."

Gabby felt the glow on Simon's face reflected in himself.

Suddenly it all fled. Simon looked down into the muddy water seeping toward them. "Then they took it away." A croak of laughter startled Gabby and the voice became bitter. "Did you know I'm a rich man, Gabby? A multi-millionaire? All of it stashed away in some bank and for that a town has good water and folks spend the afternoons paddling boats over my barn while I sit in prison. Ten years I've spent behind walls; sometimes I thought I'd turn into a lump of stone. I couldn't believe it when they sent me here where I can smell flowers again and see growing things. I couldn't stand being shut up again. But I'm still glad I did it! I'd kill more of them if I could. Drowning my land!"

Gabby couldn't move; he faced forward with a rock in his heart.

Thunder growled in the distance and clouds parted to reveal blue.

Simon shook his head and the hard mask slid from his face as he stood up and patted Gabby's shoulder. "Sorry to bend your ear like that, kid. First time I've spoke to anyone about it. Thanks for listening. Well now, look at that sunshine! We'd best get these rabbits done up for the night."

Gabby felt the empty space go cold beside him and he wished he could stay hunkered against the wall listening to Simon forever. He wanted to be able to say that he'd have killed them too. At times during his life he had wished there was somewhere other than the street to hang out in and more to home than a dark room where you ate and slept and got yelled at or sat alone wishing for someone to talk to.

He watched Simon fussing around the cages and he liked him. Liked the rounded back and the soft grey hair that fluttered in the breeze where it stuck out around his ears. He liked the way he moved, so slow and steady and he liked the soft whistle that soothed the animals while he worked. A fullness welled in Gabby's chest and when the old man turned to see why he still sat there and, instead of shouting to come and help, just smiled right from down deep in his eyes, Gabby smiled back then went over to fill water holders.

"Smell that air! So clean and fresh!" Simon straightened up and sniffed. "Seems like everything woke up and got the dust wiped off its face."

Gabby had never heard anyone say much good about rain before, but he gave a tentative sniff and was surprised to find it did smell good. He took a deep breath and then noticed that the rabbits were all sniffing too. It struck him as funny, all eight of them with eyes half closed, noses working, and he couldn't help but laugh. Then Simon laughed until the two of them had tears running down their cheeks and the rabbit's ears twitched with surprise.

Gabby's laugh was silent, but Simon's hearty bellow made enough noise for both of them and the small corner reverberated.

Two people, one who thought he had forgotten how and the other who had never learned.

From that afternoon Simon often talked when they were alone. Just long monologues, tales from his past, but he never again mentioned why he went to prison. He taught Gabby to use his eyes by pointing out things like the tiny star shaped blue flowers that struggled through the scraggly grass of the playing field. He explained Mare's Tails and Thunderhead clouds in the sky and taught him how to tell time by the sun. Even smells became important and Gabby learned that each day and each season had its own flavor.

One afternoon when the breezes were soft and sweetened by some hidden flower Gabby, with Simon along-side, pushed a wheelbarrow full of rabbit litter toward the compost heap beside the garden. A strange and beautiful sound soared from among the trees and Gabby saw a flash of gold fly up and disappear into the sun.

Simon shook his head. "There's something strange about that wood over there. I don't know what it is, but I sense something. Heard things too that oughtn't to be in woods like that. Maybe there's just some things we're not supposed to know, eh Gabby?"

Gabby had grown used to the strange night noises and his thoughts had been too involved with Simon and the rabbits to think much about the wood lately. Now, suddenly he wanted to show Simon the mysterious hair.

When they reached the pile, Gabby lowered the barrow and looked at Simon for a moment, uncertain, then he reached into the secret pouch against his ribs and carefully pulled out his treasure.

Simon's eyes shone with wonder and he came close, lightly touching the shimmering wisp with a coarsened finger. "My!" It was almost a sigh and Gabby was proud of his possession and happy that Simon appreciated it.

Together they watched the pulsing rainbow colors and after a few moments Simon spoke thoughtfully. "That's something beautiful, Gabby. You take care of it and when you find the animal it came from; you'll have found something wonderful. Keep it safe my son."

Gabby trembled with joy at the words and carefully returned the hair to its hiding place. Then Simon and he unloaded the barrow, digging rabbit litter well into the heap.

As they worked Simon whispered "My!" a few times and looked musingly into the wood, while Gabby ran over, again and again, the words "my son". Of course, he told himself, they don't mean anything, but they sure sounded nice and during the following days were never far from the back of his mind.

As summer progressed the garden flourished. Beans pulled their way up strings that had been strung for them, and beets, carrots and chard sent leaves up straight and tall. Bright orange splashes showed from groups of marigolds planted to keep insect pests away, and lettuce and radishes had already found their way to the kitchen.

Two more does gave birth and the first litter was now soft balls of fluff. Gabby was happy and refused to hear the warning voice inside him somewhere.

THE UNICORN

It was a blackberry warm day when the Unicorn first met Simon. He was carefully grazing between butterflies, cornflowers, daisies and bluebells when he reached for a snip of mint and came face to face with the two-legged one. The alien smell, so close, stunned his nostrils and froze every muscle.

The man also stood locked in shock as they stared at each other and as neither moved they began to relax. The Unicorn stretched out his neck, drawing in deep breaths as he tried to understand. Suddenly he knew; recognized the visitor from his dream, the familiar eyes and the grey beard.

Simon reached out toward the most beautiful creature he had ever seen. Like the finest horse but more stylized with a neck long and serpent like. Its legs were drawn out and delicate, but he knew they would be as strong as iron, fleet as the wind. The heavy mane seemed always moving, slowly as though each hair had life of its own, and the tail billowed like a cloud of moonlight. A glow radiated around the creature giving it an ethereal appearance and by the golden horn in the center of its forehead Simon knew what it was.

Above all else the old man saw huge eyes of burnished gold that seemed to hold the wisdom and understanding of the world. The breath smelled as sweet as the flowers of heaven and Simon saw again everything he had ever loved.

His life had been brutally unreal for so many years that this mystical creature was one thing he could believe in and he pressed his gray head against the powerful neck while tears of recognition ran down his face.

CHAPTER XV

The hall was thick with darkness as Gabby crept toward Whiteyes' cubicle for the usual Saturday meeting. The sound of whispering stopped him. He hadn't expected anyone to get here ahead of him but maybe it was a good thing. He'd always wondered how his runner talked to the gang members when he wasn't around, now he'd find out, and he prepared to listen. From the first officious words he didn't like it.

"Well, did you get anything good this week?"

"Oh hell," Gabby recognized Tod's voice, "I swiped the old I.D. tags from Tipton again."

"I thought you said you was a jewel thief!"

"I bet it's more than you got anyway. We're fed up. It's dumb stealing the same old stuff all the time. We can't keep it 'cause there's no place to stash it and 'less the helicopter comes there's nothing new. Besides it's fine for you to talk, sitting here on your tail."

Whiteyes' whisper dropped to a conspiratorial hiss. "You think I don't have something planned? If you guys weren't so eager to follow Gabby..."

"You're all talk. You don't never do nothin'."

"You smart ass punk! I'm chief around here. I don't have to prove nothin'," Whiteyes snarled obviously forgetting to whisper.

"You're only Runner. Gabby's warlord!"

"Him? He can't even talk. Where'd he be without me to give orders? You just wait ..."

Gabby wanted to kill him, right then and there, tear him limb from limb but with a mighty effort he kept self-control and told himself there were other ways without getting hung for it. He should have noticed that restlessness in the gang though. Their hunger for violence and excitement must be fed, and by him if he wanted to remain warlord. Quarrelsome voices again claimed his attention.

"It's time you proved you got some guts," Tod said defiantly.

"You know what happens if I do my thing, don't you?"

"What?"

"Gabby'll have to do his."

"So?"

Whiteyes voice flowed smooth as a snake's belly. "Gab's in here for murder; remember? I reckon he just might start with some punk kid who's rocking the boat, don't you?"

Gabby straightened as he noticed the stealthy arrival of other boys and before they saw him, he stepped through the curtain as though he had just arrived, startling Tod and Whiteyes who greeted him guiltily. The cubicle soon filled, and the meeting began.

Now Gabby was aware of the discontent, even while boys boasted of successful thefts and fights won there was a rebellious undercurrent

He wrote a note and handed it to Whiteyes. Then on second thought he took it away and handed it to Tod instead. Whiteyes would soon learn how dispensable he was!

Tod flashed a worried glance at him, then read. "Expect dangerous, exciting plan at next meeting."

As though a wind whirled through the room boredom was assuaged and the meeting ended on a note of expectation. Gabby was excited too; he didn't know what he'd come up with but he knew it would be good.

All next day the problem seethed at the back of everything he did. Even when he was with the rabbits it nagged, and as the week passed, each day went more quickly than the last, Gabby grew worried. He'd come up with lots of ideas but none quite good enough. His best had been to lead the gang in an escape but remembering the miles of forest snuffed that. Even with the arrival of Thursday night Gabby had no plan and he tossed unable to sleep. A sudden blood-curdling howl from outside sent not fear but a shot of relief through him. He had the solution to his problem, a hunt in the dark forest: The gang could spend weeks, even months, getting ready for it; making weapons, stealing supplies. When the time came most would probably be too scared to go but the challenge would bring life and purpose back to The Killers.

Gabby wrote pages of notes. Then he slept.

He welcomed Saturday eagerly. Weekends he was able to spend most of the afternoons helping Simon and today, as they cleaned pens, he listened to tales of Simon's boyhood, so different to his own it didn't seem possible. Gabby wanted to ask questions and sometimes almost tried but fear that Simon may stop talking in his comfortable, rambling way if he thought Gabby could speak, stopped him. So, he listened and conjured up pictures as they worked.

That night's meeting went as he hoped. His idea stirred the gang into a pitch of excitement and planning that sent Whiteyes into obvious gloom. The leadership he'd hoped to steal was once again secure in Gabby's grasp.

Sunday felt special from the beginning. The weight was gone from Gabby's mind, there was excitement in the future, and the afternoon to spend with Simon. When they'd first arrived, the warden had held church services, but he soon ran out of prayers, no one listened to the lessons he worked so hard to prepare and the hymns sounded like a pond full of croaking frogs, so services were quietly dropped. Now boys did chores and when they finished were allowed free time.

As soon as he could Gabby went to the rabbit hutches where he was met by Simon's grin always so welcoming, he couldn't help but grin back. They made up a new large pen and lifted the young rabbits into it, laughing as they scampered and played in their new freedom. The man and boy laughed harder as the fuzzy bodies kicked and fell over each other and neither noticed the encroaching darkness until some flies were suddenly scattered by a wind that swirled and fell quiet again. Thunder cracked overhead and the young rabbits ran, frightened, looking for their mothers. Quickly Simon and Gabby put them back in their pens to huddle behind their dams.

The wind returned, gusting and tossing Simon's words, and with it came a faint hushing sound as a curtain of rain raced across the field. The sky all at once poured water, great sheets of it and in no time Gabby's shirt clung coldly plastered to his body.

Shaking his sodden head Simon leaned close to Gabby's ear. "Follow me!" he shouted and ran into the storm.

He's gone nuts, Gabby thought as he watched the figure fade as though dissolving in the rain. For an instant it stopped and beckoned, then it was gone. Gabby shivered in dank loneliness and then he ran, pounding through new mud as rain spilled into his mouth and flooded his eyes.

Next thing he was standing breathless amid misty sunbeams with Simon smiling at him. He looked around at the brilliant greens, puzzled.

"I discovered this the other day. It's different in here." Simon pointed toward the school and it was as though a grey veil hung between them and it.

Rain still pounded onto the playing field and flashes of lightening showed trees flailing and bending in the distance, but around Gabby all was tranquil. Sunlight sifted between leaves and bluebells were scattered like fallen pieces of sky.

He turned to Simon full of questions, but the old man lay stretched out on the turf with a buttercup twining past an ear. Gabby sat down beside him.

The dreamy feeling that had suffused him before when he looked into the wood came over him again and this time, he didn't resist but lazily pulled a blade of grass, tasting its sweetness. His eyes lost focus on a sparkling water drop, a bee droned, and far away birds called.

"Gabby, Gabby."

Through tangled lashes he saw a white shape bending over him. He knew it must be the creature to which the hair belonged, the one he had almost seen twice before, and he struggled to open his eyes.

"Gabby, Gabby. It's time to go. The storm's passed."

Gabby leaped to his feet and looked eagerly around. All he saw was the white smocked figure of Simon. Surely there had been something else...

"Come lad, we don't want to be missed."

Still Gabby searched the clearing, certain that if he just looked hard enough, he'd see some sign of the elusive creature. There was nothing. Not a hoof print.

"If we cross behind the generator shack, we won't be seen," Simon was saying and Gabby followed back over the slimy field, shivering as a cold wind plucked the warmth from him.

Hurriedly they saw to the rabbits and then walked side by side toward the school door. Simon touched Gabby's sleeve before they parted. "I wouldn't let anyone else know about the wood, Gabby. They mightn't understand. Just our secret, O.K.?"

Gabby looked into Simon's earnest eyes and nodded. With a pat on Gabby's shoulder Simon was gone but Gabby stood a while, remembering. He had never dreamed anything could be so amazing. And it had spoken to him. Maybe not in words but he had heard its thoughts saying his name. It was his secret. Not even the sleeping Simon knew. Like his gossamer hair and the drumsticks, knowledge of that magical creature was his alone. Mustn't he be really special for this to have happened to him?

Filled with the importance of it he bounded up the stairs three at a time all the way to the top, and then down again to join the supper line.

Next afternoon Gabby whistled his way toward the hutches unable to resist breaking into a run as he neared the corner. He hurtled around it, grinning like a Cheshire cat, to be stopped short by a pair of surprised eyes that looked at him through wire framed glasses. The boy had Buck's cage open and poured feed into the trough Gabby had made.

Gabby only paused an instant before he ripped the trough free of the unresisting fingers.

"Cool it Gab." The boy cowered, eyes round and frightened. "The rabbits are my job now. Didn't you read the bulletin board this morning? It's first of July and all the duties are changed. I put my name down for this early and now..."

With a desperate push Gabby sent the boy sprawling, attacking with a barrage of fists but someone pulled him away and he looked into Simon's face. The sadness there made his stomach lurch.

"It's true, Gabby. I'm sorry. I tried to make them change their minds but then I'm just a prisoner too."

It must be a joke, like the time Simon limped. Gabby waited, pleading with all his soul for it to be so, but Simon's expression didn't change. Gabby heard a small voice shout gleefully in the back of his head, "I told you so, they're all the same, you can't trust anyone." And all the hurts and lessons of his past flooded in bringing black rage, like vomit, into his throat. Simon had betrayed him.

Dashing the trough to the ground Gabby ran as hard as he could into the school and up to his cubicle where he flung himself face down on the bed. He writhed in a tumult of rage and bereavement and as time passed the rage became uppermost, shutting off the cold lonely corners of his heart.

It's my own fault, he told himself, I knew better than to trust anyone and a fool to like those stupid rabbits. who needs them anyway? The more he thought about it the more he knew Simon was just a soppy old man; a man who decided he didn't like to share secrets with a kid. Sorry he showed me that place inside the wood. Afraid I'll learn more so he got rid of me. Gabby's reasoning ran through him like poison. Probably laughing at me right now. Well to hell with him!

Gabby worked and worked on his fury until it buried his disappointment. How glad he was he hadn't tried to talk. He might have told how the wood had its own moon or about the white shape he'd seen. He wished he'd never shown the hair. Maybe Simon had forgotten about it. Gabby's hurt faded to a very small ache.

He became aware of a sound. Music that soothed and threatened the wall he had built, and he stormed down the hallway, following the wavering chords to a cubicle where a boy played his harmonica. The tune that had laughed and danced around the walls now ended in a wail as Gabby knocked the instrument from between lip and hand to crash against the dresser.

After a curse the boy sat scared, blood running down his chin. He saw the fury in Gabby's eyes and recoiled from it. "Okay, okay. I won't play again."

The image of his fear stayed with Gabby as he left. That was the way everyone must look at him from now on, they'd never find a soft spot in him again.

The following days were one sour ball of anger and only the satisfaction of being Warlord made them bearable. He had checked the bulletin board and in bold new letters it stated, SISKIN-SWEEP FRONT HALL AND KITCHEN DUTY.

Gabby gnawed on his grievances as a dog its bone. While he swept the hall, he railed against being treated as a servant. If I was anywhere else, he thought, I could write to the papers. But he was nowhere and there was no one to tell or to care. He hated every face, hated the smells that hung in different rooms, hated the squeak of the second stair to the top. Above all he hated the sound of the bell, always rung at the same times, ordering him about. He stepped on every tiny flower he saw in the field and ignored the garden. As he did dishes after supper the smell of the water made him gag and he wished he could drown the fat cook in it.

He pretended not to see Simon the few times their paths crossed and never looked to the far table where he sat at mealtime. If he had seen the hurt in the old man's face, he probably wouldn't have recognized it, his shield of anger was so thick.

One evening when he looked from his window, he thought he saw a shape slip in among the trees but though he watched for a long time he didn't see it emerge. He firmly kept his thoughts away from the wood and the hair securely trapped beneath his drumsticks.

Only if he relaxed did his mind stray to things forbidden and once, with a pile of greasy dishes in front of him his eyes were drawn like a pair of moths to a distant glow outside the window. He imagined Simon sitting on fresh grass with rainbows flickering around him and in the shadow behind stood an awesome luminescent shape. Gabby could almost see what it was…He smashed a glass down on the counter and a chunk flew up and cut his shoulder. He watched the blood run down his arm and into the soon pink dishwater.

THE UNICORN

The Unicorn and the old man spent much time together, for as often as possible Simon escaped to the Mystical Wood. He wished he need never return to the school but knowledge of the search that would follow his disappearance always forced him back. He could not be the cause of leading all that evil into the wood.

He had wanted to bring the boy again. Something about the child had drawn him from the beginning, perhaps the desperate fierceness like a cornered wolf cub. He had almost reached the soft spot he felt lay so deeply hidden — then it had all been spoiled and they were lost to each other. Perhaps the Unicorn was the one creature that could save him, humans could never do it now. Simon looked into the wise golden eyes and prayed that it might be so.

CHAPTER XVI

"**M**ove it, boy. No time for daydreaming here."

Gabby snapped back to the muggy kitchen and Cook who pointed to a bucket of potato peelings to be thrown out. Picking it up he slouched toward the cans outside, taking care not to look in the direction of the rabbits, trying not to breathe familiar smells. Whiffs that did get through caused a small pain somewhere deep inside and, quickly dumping his load, he rushed back to the kitchen. As he finished the dishes, he pictured how Simon would laugh to see him up to the elbows in suds and he wished he could think of some way to pay him back for being a traitor; and a rotten bastard. It was all the teachers could do to get any work at all out of Gabby and soon they decided it wasn't worth the effort and left him alone. In woodworking he carved sharp pointy objects and then broke them. In free time he organized ball games and urged the teams into wild battles though most complained it was getting too warm. Gabby insisted they get fit for the hunt and with that in mind they complied. He put his all into those games and on the endless weekends he made the boys play until they could run no farther.

On a Saturday night, aching and bruised, they met, grumbling and snapping at each other even after the meeting had started.

"I stole this." Tod flashed a gold ring.

"Big deal. I stole it last week. Belongs to the bald teacher." Fang whispered back.

"But I stole it right off his hand," Tod retorted.

"Like hell you did."

Before blows erupted Gabby signaled for Beauty to give out whatever it was he held and, when it turned out to be Ritz crackers, the groan of disappointment could have been heard down the hall. Even so, each boy dutifully took his share, or more if he could get it, and the only sound was munching.

As they ate, Gabby tried to think of something to spark excitement. The hunt was fine, but they needed something now. Next to him Whiteyes' chewing got louder and more disgusting until Gabby wanted to punch him in the mouth. He stared angrily at the piggy face and suddenly had an idea which he wrote and handed to his runner who turned to him in alarm. "Hey, Gabby, we don't have to do this."

Gabby insisted Whiteyes read the note aloud.

"Gabby says he and I are to have a competition. Whichever of us does the worst thing by next Saturday is winner.

"Hey, Gabby, y'know..."

But already the boys had latched onto the idea. They tossed it around like a football, guessing wildly as to the winner's crime. Enjoying the thought of competition between their top members. Whiteyes saw he had no way out and agreed.

Back in his cubicle Gabby excitedly beat his muted drumsticks. He looked forward to showing Whiteyes up once and for all and had no doubt he would think of something that would stun everyone. He dreamed and twitched like a dog all night.

The gang was on tenterhooks all the next day trying to watch the two rival's every move, but it wasn't till Tuesday that Whiteyes slipped away from them all. The first anyone knew of his accomplishment was when Warden burst into the dining room in a cloud of anger and perturbation. Every boy stopped chewing and waited expectantly.

"This morning someone destroyed the vegetable garden. I didn't think anyone would stoop so low as to vandalize something so important to us all."

The gasp that rose from the listeners was partially dismay but Gabby could tell that from the gang it was admiration as surreptitiously they looked from Gabby to Whiteyes wondering which to credit. The flush blotching the usual pallor of the Runner's cheeks gave him away and he shot a triumphant glance toward Gabby.

Gabby ignored him and ate on, unconcerned, but inwardly the gasp had sounded like a cheer and now he churned and sifted ideas seeking one to top his rival.

"Will the culprit step forward?" Warden perched on his toes like a hawk ready to dive. He barely paused, knowing no one would confess. "All free time is hereby cancelled. When not fulfilling an assignment, you must stay in your cubicles. Anyone caught wandering will be beaten. And no sports"

He sat down with an angry thump.

Maybe I wasn't so smart to let that fink go first, thought Gabby, he's sure made it a lot more difficult for me. He glanced at the others and hoped they realized this, then he thought how much more they would think of his winning against such odds. But would they hold it against Whiteyes that they had to suffer for what he did.

As he left the room, he ignored Whiteyes' smug looks and made it plain he was not impressed.

Fang shuffled up beside him, "Wow that was really something, eh?"

Gabby shrugged and curled his lip, refusing to look at the garden as they passed it on the way to the workshop. He remembered raking the soft earth.

"You got to admit it'll be about impossible to beat, won't it? I reckon Whiteyes won the competition. You got to be really dirty to do something like that."

Blabber mouthed fool, Gabby thought, and his fist shot out leaving Fang to nurse a bloody nose.

A short while later Whiteyes made an excuse to work next to him and Gabby's back stiffened to hear preliminary throat clearing. "How's that then, Gab? You couldn't have done it, could you? I've seen you. You get soft over things. Couldn't have hurt your old string beans." With a croaking laugh Whiteyes moved quickly away as Gabby's knife slashed viciously through the wood he worked.

It wasn't until after supper when the others were confined to their cubicles and Gabby was at work in the kitchen that he managed to get a look at the garden. He took the garbage out and after dumping it dodged quickly around the corner and over to the ravaged plot. It looked like a battlefield. Broken and pulled up stakes lay tangled among remains of wilted bean stalks and tomato plants. Carrots chopped into fleshy orange chunks mixed with the blood of beets, and hacked off lettuce heads lay trampled into the earth. A cabbage balanced high on a stake like a decapitated head and beneath it puffs of marigold straggled like drops of gore. Already it smelled like garbage and Gabby watched shiny black flies circle and settle and buzz.

He felt sick but he couldn't stop watching. A faint sound startled him and he turned to see Simon with a bucket come to salvage what he could for the rabbits.

"Hello, Gabby."

Gabby wanted to run but all he could do was stare into the familiar, gentle face. The face that had pretended to be a friend. All the hurt rose again.

"How are you doing, Gabby? We miss you."

The voice soughed like a soft wind in the trees, carrying tenderness that formed a lump in Gabby's throat.

Like hell you miss me! You made them change the schedule or you could have stopped them. I hate you, I hate you! The unspoken words stabbed at the lump. A lot you miss me, you lying old bastard! Still he stared into the kind eyes and fought the temptation to believe them.

Smells of decay surrounded them. Garbage. Everything turned to garbage. That's all life was. Gabby looked down at the destruction and, full of disgust, ran back to the kitchen where he brooded over Simon's deception. He banged pots and pans as though the noise could dull the raw hurt from which the scab had been newly torn. Again, he bandaged it in rage and longed for revenge.

He turned the tap on full and with water an idea poured. An idea by which he could pay both his enemies off at once; Simon and Whiteyes in one swoop. For the rest of the day if someone spoke to him, he didn't hear. He went from place to place like a sleepwalker and pushed boys out of his way without seeing them. The solution was a needle ready to puncture the boil of his bitterness and single mindedly he looked toward the hour of accomplishment.

Gabby lay still and tense as the guard made his final bed check. He waited until the whole world seemed asleep and counted as the distant clock chimed midnight. Still he waited. Someone cried out in a nightmare and Gabby listened for another eternity in case a guard came to investigate. At last he got out of bed fully dressed and crept across the wooden floor and downstairs. The guard slumped across his desk, finger still through the handle of his half-emptied coffee mug. He gave a jolting snore as Gabby passed.

The kitchen corridor was clogged with smells of past dinners and Gabby gulped the fresh air that hit his face when he stepped out into the silent night. There was no noise at all, not even from the wood, and a small moon rolled in and out of silver rimmed sheep backs of cloud. Gabby walked resolutely to where the cages quietly waited and rabbit eyes watched from fuzzy bodies made into jigsaw puzzles by shadows of netting. In momentary betrayal Gabby's nose sniffed once enjoyed smells but his mind saw Whiteyes' mocking smirk and heard the nasal voice say, "You get soft over things." He remembered how Simon had gotten rid of him and how the world was garbage.

His fingers opened the first cage and reached in, feeling until they grasped the soft rabbit neck that pushed trustingly against them. Taking hold his hands twisted. A crack, the warm body kicked and went limp. Gabby moved on from cage to cage and as each neck cracked, he thought of everything that had ever let him down. Heard his mother yell for him to shut up and go away, saw distorted faces scream their anger at him, as each rabbit body lay killed in hate.

In the final cage Buck sat, head up, waiting. Gabby envisioned Simon snuggling the big rabbit against his cheek. Simon the traitor. With a chop of his hand behind quivering ears, Buck crumpled and to Gabby it was Simon lying there, unable to ever tell him to go away again.

A dawn hinting gust swayed the row of open cage doors and Gabby, suddenly weary, turned and made his way back to his cubicle, the darkness having turned into a jelly like sea for him to wade through. Tired beyond belief, he fell onto his bed and down a well of sleep.

CHAPTER XVII

Gabby awoke with the empty feeling of something wrong. But no- slowly a kernel of excitement uncurled then, as though a floodgate lifted, triumphant thoughts whirled. He'd won: Had paid them all back, all of them, and firmly established his position as Warlord at the same time. He couldn't wait to see Whiteyes' expression when he heard and realized how feeble it made his destruction of the garden look. Why his was like being a greengrocer compared to this!

Impatiently Gabby waited. Surely recognition must come soon. The wakeup bell rang, sounding no different than on any other morning. But, of course, it was too early for anyone to have found the rabbit carcasses yet.

All the time he washed and dressed Gabby's ears felt they would peel away from his head with their effort to catch the first shout or sound of running feet.

It was the boy with glasses who first brought word to the warden. Running in in the middle of breakfast, red faced and bawling, he whispered, and Warden followed him outside. Suddenly Gabby was hungry and reached for two pieces of bread and poured more milk. As he drank, he caught Whiteyes' looking at him over the rim of his glass and gave a huge wink.

Soon every boy in the room knew that whatever had happened was done by one of them, but the gang knew it was Gabby and fidgeted to find out what it was.

It was horribly frustrating for Gabby to be in the kitchen when the news did get out and, as dishes clinked in and out of his hands, he imagined the excitement. Hardly knowing what he did he picked up the bag of garbage and went outside with it. Quietly he put it in the can and found himself taking the few extra steps to the corner and carefully looking around it. Ugly green flies circled the doorways to silent hutches and, sitting on the ground, back toward him, Simon cradled Buck in his arms. The rounded shoulders rocked slowly back and forth, the rabbit's head swinging, ears flopping limply, until Gabby was almost mesmerized. Back and forth. Back and forth. Something fell and glistened in the fur.

Suddenly Simon looked around and it was like a dash of scalding water as Gabby faced the grieving eyes. For a moment man and boy stared at each other and try as he would Gabby could not feel the triumph he wanted. Breakfast rose in his craw and he turned and slunk away.

To stop from thinking, Gabby lost himself in the cacophony of colliding pots and pans until Cook was glad to get rid of him. Then he ran to receive congratulations from The Killers. Their effusive praise made Gabby lightheaded and all morning he walked among pats on the back and flashed thumbs up while Whiteyes skulked, defeated, in the background.

The bell for afternoon classes was unusually late. Gabby sat cross legged on his bed and munched the chocolate bar left by Beauty. It had been wrapped in a note which Gabby read for the second time, "Hooray, I knew you'd win." He had thrown it away once but then retrieved it and now stuffed it in his secret place under the floorboards.

He was impatient to get back with the gang for more deserved adulation but at the same time he expected to be called down to the warden's office. Surely Simon had told on him by now. He knew. Gabby could see it in the eyes that had met his that morning. He must have told. They were probably planning what to do to him; that's what the holdup was.

Gabby checked the sun. It was well after one o'clock. They surely must be having some meeting about him. A roar crept up and engulfed him and he leaped to the window to see the helicopter's familiar shape lower to the field. So that's what they'd been waiting for, not discussing him at all!

The same two men who always came worked quietly but this time Gabby wasn't interested and just stayed at the window out of habit.

Everything unloaded, the engine started, but still the machine waited. Gabby wondered why and then something jolted inside him as he saw the solitary bent figure of Simon walk across the field. As he watched a cold fog shivered through his soul and he drew a sharp breath at the misery in it. Barely breathing he saw the frail body beaten by wind from the whirling blades, and his hands grasped the window bars, quivering with the intensity of their hold. Arms pulled Simon inside, the door shut, and the helicopter lifted Skyward.

Gabby's eyes followed until the helicopter disappeared. "I couldn't stand being locked up again." He heard Simon's voice, and now there was only silence, a pile of boxes in the field, and himself empty and alone.

"Wow, man that was something else!"

Unnoticed the gang had crowded into his cubicle and now stood looking at him.

"Yeah man, you're really something." Tod spoke, flushed with enthusiasm. "Fancy planning it all for helicopter day so's you got rid of the old guy too and we won't have to fix up that stupid garden." He paused as Gabby didn't move. "It's O.K. The guards are all outside checking over their new liquor supply."

Gabby stared into the idolizing faces and shook his head. The cold left him, melted by the warmth of praise. He was a god as happy and proud he stepped down among his worshippers.

CHAPTER XVIII

Summer dropped over the school like a suffocating blanket. Boys and men moved in festering boredom and quarrels rankled and broke out like small fires to quickly die through lack of energy.

At first Gabby had waited for some reaction from the warden to his killing of the rabbits, but nothing happened. It puzzled him until one day Pirate met him on the stairs.

"Hey, Gabby, guess what, I just heard Warden tell Tyler he was glad the garden and rabbits was killed. Seems he thought they was a waste of time all along and was glad of the chance to get rid of Simon. I guess we was lucky or we'd all have been skinned for sure!"

Pigs, thought Gabby hating the men even more.

"And they don't know it was you done it either. I could tell the way they talked."

Pirate's news left Gabby strangely bothered. Why hadn't Simon told on him? It was a worrisome thought and he kept having to shrug it out of his mind like it was a biting fly.

Day followed day in the semblance of curriculum, but the boys had no interest in learning and the teachers knew there was no point to their teaching. The building seemed airless and it was feared the well might go dry, so showers were rationed to one a week per boy. Each cherished the few moments allotted to standing under the cool rush of water and bartered their turns only for a high price.

Allowed no sports, the boys spent many hours sitting miserably in their cubicles waiting for summer to pass while outside the field simmered, baked brown, imprisoning the humans in their island of shade.

Gabby tried, against all odds, to keep the gang meetings interesting and they remained the only bright spot. Once he found a fifth of whiskey hidden in a corner of the kitchen and smuggled it to The Killers who imbibed it amid choking and gleeful chuckles. That was the best meeting of all, but everyone felt terrible next day.

After weeks of relentless sun-scorched boredom no one could say a civil word. The school was a pressure cooker and each boy a firecracker that only waited for the right spark to ignite it.

On an endless Saturday afternoon Gabby sprawled semi- naked across his bed and tried to imagine that a breeze blew through the window. He had broken the glass early in the hot spell when he found it only opened a few inches, but it made no difference. His mouth tasted like cardboard and he wondered if it was worth the trouble to get his drumsticks from their hiding place in the floor. It was too hot to wear them these days.

He wondered when the helicopter was due again. It had come twice since Simon left and each time Gabby half expected to see a smocked figure begin to unload hutches. But it never happened, and he would turn away emptier than before.

"What's that you got?"

Gabby jumped to see Whiteyes in his cubicle doorway and followed the direction in which the pale eyes looked. He saw that his hands had unconsciously taken out the hair from his pouch and had twisted it around his palm until his fingers were swollen red. He shrugged and shook it loose, letting it fall to the floor as though it were nothing. He should have known Whiteyes wouldn't let it go at that and he tightened with irritation to see the loathed hands reach to pick it up. He wished the hair wouldn't shimmer as Whiteyes held it to the light. He hated the way the greedy hands touched and pulled his property. Pretending not to care he inwardly seethed and longed for his enemy to lose interest and drop it.

"Jeeze, what is this?" Whiteyes searched Gabby's face.

Why should I want a dumb old hair anyway, Gabby thought as in an agony of frustration he watched Whiteyes stuff it into his own pocket? It took all his control not to jump up and snatch it back but instead he stared at the hot sky through his window and tried not to think of the way Simon had said, "My!" when he'd seen it.

He felt Whiteyes leave and suddenly he missed Simon more than he'd ever missed anything. His chest hurt with the pain of it and he squeezed his eyes tight shut and clenched his fists. Sitting up he grasped the drumsticks and beat on the dark skin of his thigh. Smack. Smack. This pain chased the other and sweat poured like tears.

He beat harder and harder and all at once a light flashed around the room followed by a crash of thunder. Jumping onto his bed Gabby looked out into a grid of rain that lashed the ground with innumerable whips. Thunder clapped and shook the building and Gabby heard frightened cries from the cubicles around him. He loved the storm, leaning closer to the window to feel splashes on his face from the rain that ricocheted off the bars. Excitedly he leaped to the floor and then around the room beating with his drumsticks the dresser, bed and walls. Adding to the tumult outside, he beat with all his strength, bursting with power, invincible. His cannonade on the metal bed rail grew louder and faster and carried him away on the sound and fury of it.

"What the hell's all this about?" The guard in his doorway bellowed.

Gabby, riding the crest of the storm, ignored the man and jumped onto the bed to beat a wild tattoo on the window bars. A heavy blow toppled him back to the floor and the drumsticks clattered from his grasp. He pounced after them but the guard already had them in his hand and inspected them with a grin. He looked at Gabby and, staring into his furious eyes, carefully broke each stick in half. Then he laughed.

Blackness closed in on Gabby as with a soundless roar he leaped at the mocking face, gouging, clawing, kicking. Caught off guard the big man backed into the hall, but Gabby was on him with all the wildcat fury of his fourteen years. Half smothered by the smell of stale sweat he felt soft flesh give and push under his blows and the sound of the storm was the sound of their battle. He wanted nothing but to fight until the mountain beneath him lay still. Other bodies joined them, but Gabby kicked to keep them away. This was his prey. But he couldn't stop them and soon was surrounded and then submerged by hoarsely breathing boys who reached and clawed for the guard beneath him.

Gabby fought his way free and stood apart watching the struggling tangled mass, lit now and again by flashes of lightening. It surged up and down the corridor, banging into walls on either side and a deep inhuman roar joined the thunder. Boys kept coming, eyes bright and eager as they threw themselves into the writhing knot, clawing for its bleeding nucleus.

The nightmarish scene seemed no longer connected to Gabby and he returned to his cubicle and picked up the broken drumsticks. For a moment he looked at them, then stroked them clean and slid the shattered pieces back into their pouch where they almost looked whole again. After strapping them to their familiar place against his ribs he pulled on shirt and jeans.

The rain had stopped leaving an uncanny silence. Sounds of running feet. Then again dead quiet.

Gabby slowly sat down on his bed.

It seemed a long time before he heard voices far away at the foot of the stairs. "My God! What have they done to him?"

"Torn apart ... All the blood ... Nothing but animals. Get him to bed." The words floated, disembodied.

Gabby smiled and lay back stroking the drumsticks under his shirt. He wondered what the men would do now.

Nothing happened and no sound came from any cubicle. The sun came out and slid into dusk and Gabby fell asleep. When he awoke it was dark and his stomach gave a hollow growl.

He got up and looked into the hall. The boy opposite did the same and further down the row other curtains moved. A strange smell hung in the air.

Sure there were no guards about, Gabby left his cubicle. Others joined him and a soft whispering began. Boys padded up from the floor below with news that there was no sign of men anywhere and a carefree mood grew. Someone laughed and soon everyone was talking.

A voice called through the hubbub. "Where's our chief? Where's Gabby?"

From nearby Gabby heard, "He's here! He's here!"

He felt twenty-nine boys surge toward him and saw their arms reach out. As hands touched him Gabby felt panic and saw again the weaving, boy-covered body of the guard, then he found himself pushed ahead of them and fear gave a dying shudder. It changed to exultation as he heard shouts.

"Hail to our warlord! Chief killer of The Killers!"

Soon it became a chant and a noisy dance swayed up and down the hall.

"Trust Gabby to come up with something good."

"This was even better than the rabbits."

"Good old Gabby! Wonder what his next plan will be. He gets better every time for sure."

Excited chatter surrounded him and hearing the praise Gabby realized everyone thought he had planned the attack for their amusement. Soon he thought he had.

They stopped and he saw that now every boy in the school waited for him to guide their next move. He almost choked with exaltation and fervently wished Skull could see him now.

Where were the men? Gabby realized he must do something. His stomach came to the rescue and with a sweep of his arm he began to run, the rest close on his heels, downstairs and into the kitchen. The light when they turned it on was startling after so much darkness and the boys blinked for a moment, then separated to forage through cupboards and refrigerator, tearing at chunks of meat, gnawing cheese and throwing what they had aside for something that looked better.

Gabby commandeered a dishpan full of chocolate pudding and leaned over it with a serving spoon making fast heaping trips to his mouth. The richness slid luxuriously down his throat and his eyes half closed in rapture. His arm grew slower as his stomach grew tighter, but he couldn't stop with half the pan still full. He forced more down. Spots wavered before his eyes and suddenly Gabby never wanted to see chocolate pudding again. He let the spoon submerge sluggishly in the brown mess and bolted from the kitchen to press his forehead against a wall in the darkness of the hall.

As dizziness subsided, he became aware of the line of light under the warden's door and automatically he sidled toward it and pressed his ear against the panels. It surprised him to hear men's voices, somehow, he'd thought them all vanished.

A wave of nausea attacked and the conversation in the room sounded muzzy but after a moment or two he was able to understand.

"I said in the beginning there weren't enough of us."

"More men would mean less money."

"He's right. Bob was careless. Forgot what savages these kids are. From now on keep your guns handy and don't be afraid to use them."

Gabby didn't try to sort out who spoke, and the words washed around his head.

"I still think we should report the attack. Bob was darn lucky not to be killed."

"Oh hell! You know they'd close the place if word got out about something like this. I need the money and so do you or, let's face it, we wouldn't have signed up for time in this end of the world joint. Just keep your trigger fingers ready, think of you bank account and..."

Vertigo zoomed through Gabby's system and he just made it to the nearest bathroom in time.

Five minutes later he again stood in the hall weak but no longer nauseous. He even felt the return of hunger, though definitely not for anything chocolate, and soon he was back in the kitchen happily gorging on strawberry jam.

CHAPTER XIX

Gabby awoke early and had he been one of the Roosters Simon used to talk about he would have crowed. He was the most important person in the whole school!

Again and again he ran over yesterday's happenings; the attack, the celebration and the feast, but mostly he heard the praise. He grew on it and swore he would do anything to keep his position.

He breathed deeply of the rain freshened air and smiled to hear the bell rung so angrily: as though the hand on it wished it wrung the necks of the boys it wakened. He thought of the guns the men would be wearing and welcomed their show of force. It would be like in the comics. Everyone was scared of Gabby, warlord of The Killers. Wow, he was really something all right!

He looked at himself in the mirror as he dressed and put an extra high wave in his hair. Not till he figured everyone was downstairs did he follow, and then he clumped noisily, making a grand entrance before his faithful followers who crowded to greet him.

But they were not looking at him. Instead they seemed hypnotized by the firearms blatantly displayed by seven men at the top end of the room. Boys stood in shuffling groups, all last night's bravado gone, their hero seemingly forgotten.

Well they'll see I'm not scared by any old guns. Gabby barged his way to the back wall where he leaned picking his teeth with a broom straw.

Warden stopped talking to the men and looked at his audience with eyes like skinned gooseberries. "You ought to all be hung for yesterday's performance. Almost murdered that guard you did; for two pins I'd send you back to a regular reformatory."

But you won't, thought Gabby. We're money to you.

"Instead I'm going to work your butts off and any kid who starts anything like last night, even hints of it, will be disposed of. You'll be treated like the animals you are." After spitting his last words Warden left the room, his men trailing behind him.

Gabby felt his power evaporate. The kids should be looking to him for guidance. He searched for a way to shake their apathy, anything to make them focus on him again.

Warden had called them animals. Okay. Gabby leaped to the front, threatening with great claws, tossing his head and snarling like a tiger.

Fang caught his message and followed, swaggering like a great ape. "I'm a ferocious animal," he shouted, "Warden says so!"

Soon others caught the spirit and followed, snorting, braying and roaring. The spell was broken. Anxiety fled and laughter took over until boys laughed and collapsed in hysterical release.

When Gabby reported for kitchen duty even he was surprised at the chaos caused by the night's invasion, and then he cursed his luck to be working here on this of all days. At least he could have a good laugh at Cook who wore an incongruous black holster over his apron and didn't know where to put his hands because of it. The fat man nervously watched Gabby's every move and Gabby played with his fear, moving suddenly just to see him jump. It almost made up for the unpleasantness of scraping chocolate pudding off the floor into which it had been trampled and scrubbing the filthy counter of its unrecognizable mess.

His teacher, Gabby found in class later, was in the similar nervous state as Cook - fidgeting and afraid to turn his back on the roomful of boys. Gabby mocked his fear and shook and rolled his eyes for the benefit of the class when the man's attention was elsewhere.

Sweat beaded the teacher's nose as he strove to ignore the outbursts of giggles. Having orders to use the ultimate weapon he seemed to have lost his intermediary powers of discipline and the boys very soon became adept at knowing just how far they could go. Instead of a war of guns it became a war of nerves.

After class every chore possible was thought up to keep the boys busy. Gabby had the easiest time as it was an honor to be allowed to do his work for him and boys fought for the privilege. While they did double, he strode the halls like an admired dictator and though the staff watched him warily they left him alone.

The boys enjoyed their baiting and games with the staff for about a week, after which chaos became a bore and they felt like stones being tumbled in the same small space.

Hot weather returned. It didn't seem fair to have a repeat of all they had suffered before and this time it seemed even worse. Depression weighted everyone.

One scorching afternoon a fly buzzed hopelessly at the window as background to the reading voice of the teacher. Gabby idly picked splinters from his chewed pencil and made neither head nor tail of the poetry floating over his head. Sissy stuff. He noticed that at least four kids seemed to be asleep. He slumped lower in his chair watching the fly always just miss the opening it sought. What he wouldn't give for a cool breath of air and mentally he reached for a breeze though he knew there was none.

"Oh go and sit with her and be o'er shaded under the languid downfall of her hair."

The words isolated themselves and flashed like neon in Gabby's mind. They triggered a need that shot him to his feet and sent him from the room, ignoring the teacher's shout. He ran upstairs, two at a time, straight to Whiteyes' cubicle. There he pulled out drawers and sent clothes and dirty socks flying. He looked under the mattress and behind the mirror. He felt the floor for loose boards and dipped his fingers in the water jug. Not finding what he sought he grew frantic. What if Whiteyes had thrown it away! He couldn't! Despairing, Gabby gave one last look around and this time saw a spark.

The hair twined casually around the foot rail of the bed and as Gabby reached it seemed to fall into his hand. How familiar and good it felt! He held it against his cheek and a cool breeze brushed his face bringing thoughts he had tried to forget. A strange feeling prickled his throat and behind his eyes. Carefully Gabby folded the hair safely into the pouch he had worn since the night of the storm and pushed the broken drumsticks in beside it it.

He felt at ease as he returned downstairs and the heat didn't seem nearly as bad. He was whistling as he met the others leaving class and hungrily ate his own lunch and another boy's. He must have been the only one in the whole dining room with any appetite at all.

"What the hell did you rip up my place for?" Whiteyes asked as they entered class later. "What were you looking for? I don't have nothing you'd want."

Gabby was surprised at no mention of the hair. It seemed Whiteyes hadn't even missed it. Probably forgotten all about it. Idiot! Quickly he scribbled; Security. Thought they might bug meeting.

Whiteyes read the note, frowned, then his face cleared. "Hey, good thought. Find anything?"

Gabby shook his head and went to collect carving tools. Some kids were sure dumb. He forgot Whiteyes and concentrated on the wood he shaped into the face of a horse with very large eyes.

It didn't seem possible to get hotter, but it did and the sun hung ready to pounce on any living thing and shrivel it to nothing. To escape the wretchedness, Gabby became obsessed by the hair, imagining it brought relief from some cool place just out of sight and if only he tried hard enough, he could be there.

He watched it in the privacy of his room and slept with it in his hand at night.

One afternoon it had the fragrance of fresh grass and Gabby remembered the taste of the blade he had chewed in the wood so long ago. A great craving grew for that sweetness on his tongue again and he looked to where the trees wavered on the other side of the playing field's trembling heat curtain. Suddenly he could no longer stand the suffocating walls that crowded him and, putting the hair in his pouch, padded unnoticed downstairs and out into the unbreathable furnace of the field. At first, he expected to be called back but as no command came, he realized the guards had no thought beyond their own discomfort and he forgot them as the sun attacked.

It sucked the air from his lungs and made his temples throb. Clothes clung and his feet burned so that each step was more painful than the last. There was no sound and no movement but his own. Gabby wanted to turn back, but something pulled him on - and then he stood among ferns, washed by a tide of cool air. Gasping, he lifted his arms, closed his eyes and raised his face. For a long time, he stayed that way then he opened his eyes and looked into leaves that stirred and sifted light and dark greens. Their brightness amazed him; for a long time, life had seemed colorless, almost black and white.

Birdsong trembled about him and a shadow swooped across the ground, touched his shoulder and was gone. Heart beating with excitement, Gabby pushed into the dusk of tall trees and leaped for a branch from which he swung, legs kicking, laughing. Energy flowing through every cell as he dropped to the ground and ran, trailing his hands over trunks, pulling leaves. He snapped twigs and tore tufts of thistle- down, jumped over rocks and trampled daisies. His head bobbed from side to side, up and down, looking, searching, peering.

A tall stem supported a giant Sunflower and Gabby broke it off and studied the nubby green-brown face. He pulled the golden petals, soft as mouse fur; twirled and twisted them until they lost their captured sunshine and looked raggedy and sad.

The sound of running water took his attention and he followed it to a tiny stream fed pool. Casting the sunflower onto the surface he watched it spread and grow perfect again. Lazily it turned, its shadow drifting over the chestnut colored clay beneath.

Intrigued by the pool's clarity Gabby kneeled, nose close to the surface. A small fish darted. Gabby's hand flashed after it, raising angry swirls of mud. The murky water reminded him of mud puddles in the city and he wondered if any of them hid fish. As the water cleared, he began to notice tiny creatures; a beetle with red wings, tiny flies that skimmed the pond's surface almost touching, big insects with transparent blue wings, and swimming things slender as the tip of a needle.

An emerald frog swam nonchalantly, hands at its sides, long legs working. Gabby almost expected it to hum and grinned at its serious expression. He would have caught it but didn't know whether frogs bit or stung or something.

A faint path tempted him off to the left and he became an Indian, moving on stealthy moccasined feet. His soundlessness pleased him, and he broke off tall stalks topped by silken white fronds to carry as spears. Now he ran, beating everything he passed so he left a trail of white pieces. His lance left no damage but its own and finally, out of breath, Gabby hurled it into the heart of some beast who lurked in the shadows of his mind.

A tree blocked his way and seeing the inviting vine that twined about its trunk he became Tarzan and scampered up to sit high on a limb. Gabby had climbed many a flimsy fire escape to tenement rooftops, but the view he now saw was very different. Trees stretched to the horizon in puffs of multi-shaded greens, so soft and rounded he felt he could step down and walk on them, but when he turned the other way he faced a shimmering wall, hot and forbidding, and deep within it floated a dark shape that swayed and jiggled. It was a few moments before Gabby recognized the school and he looked with fascination from his cool perch.

Rustle. Rustle. Gabby's thoughts jumped back to his tree. Below he glimpsed a disappearing shadow and flung himself after it, sliding, swinging, until he lost hold and tumbled from branch to branch to land on a mattress of pine needles. Springing to his feet he saw nothing to follow. Probably a bird, he decided, and sat down with his back against warm bark. Dreamily content he watched a butterfly land on a blue flower, wings upright, pulsing and quivering.

A harsh clatter shattered the peace. Distant but jarring it disturbed the wood and Gabby was angry the school bell should reach him here. Grudgingly he obeyed its summons, retracing his steps, until he came to the lonely sunflower stalk, now barren, with nothing to show the sun. He paused, wishing the flower was still there.

At the Wood's edge he looked carefully through ferns to make sure he was unseen before stepping onto the field. The forgotten heat nearly knocked him backward, but he forced himself forward under the crushing weight of it and wiped the sweat that ran into his eyes. By the time he entered the building his visit to the wood seemed a faint dream and he wondered if maybe his brain had melted. Perhaps it had all been a mirage though he wasn't quite sure what a mirage was.

"Hey, what's that all over you? Where've you been anyway?" Whiteyes looked him up and down and Gabby saw that filmy white flecks clung to his clothes. He brushed them to the floor, whirling and spinning like motes of light before they disappeared. Whiteyes tried to catch one but it vanished as it touched his hand. Gabby watched, jubilant. It hadn't been a mirage! Everything was real and his own secret.

Soon he dove into his plate of hot dogs, mashed potatoes and sauerkraut. Hungrily he scarfed them and not until he finished, did he notice the many questioning eyes on him. Word had gotten around that he'd been somewhere. He'd have to tell the gang something and as he ate apple crumble, he decided to write that he'd been exploring the forest in preparation for the hunt. They'd never connect it with his own wood if he was careful never to be seen entering or leaving it.

"Where'd you go?" Tod stopped him outside the dining room.

Gabby grinned the kind of grin that meant he knew something special. The kind meant to tantalize and frustrate those who waited for an answer.

He gave the sign for "meeting tonight" then strolled toward the homework room where he hunched over smudgy paper alternately writing and chewing his pencil.

CHAPTER XX

The deafening creak of the second step from the top rooted Gabby to where he stood in the hushed darkness of the stairwell. He waited tensely for the arrival of the guards but when they didn't come, he let out his breath and cautiously continued upward.

Tonight's would be the first meeting of The Killers since the attack on the guard who, still bandaged, now sat with his mate in the hall below. There were always two on duty now; trigger happy and boy hating. Gabby relished the extra danger as he crept along the stifling corridors.

As soon as he reached Whiteyes' cubicle the meeting began with Pirate relegated to guard the doorway. All anybody wanted was to hear Gabby's notes and they listened raptly as Whiteyes read. Even Gabby was entranced by his made-up story.

"Today I went into the forest so I'll know where to find animals when we go on the hunt. It was pitch dark and things watched from behind trees. I heard them growl. Had to fight through bushes and run snakes out of my way. Vultures sat in treetops and I saw lots of monsters but didn't let them see me. One big white bear though, he took after me and I had to run like hell to keep ahead of his teeth that must have been a foot long."

There was a lot more and Gabby felt braver and prouder of himself the longer he listened. He was sorry when Whiteyes finished and wished he had left in the part about killing the tiger. The cubicle was hushed as listeners digested the tale, throwing away splinters of disbelief and keeping the knowledge of slight exaggeration. Gabby saw himself as the game hunter in the cigarette billboard above Joe's pool hall, and around him sat his slaves.

"Wow, weren't you scared?" Beauty's voice trembled from his corner.

Gabby shrugged.

"Are you going back ever? I mean if it's so bad." It was another voice and Gabby knew they were all thinking of the time they must enter that dark scary place.

He nodded a vigorous affirmative and quickly wrote. "Must, so you won't all be eaten on the first hunt." It gave him pleasure to hear it said and feel the dark quiver with fear as his followers recoiled from the thought.

Tod released the tension. "We've a lot to do before we're anyways ready to go. 'Sides it's too hot yet."

A hum of agreement followed.

"Guard!" Pirate's frantic whisper made everyone scurry for cover.

Whiteyes plunged under the blankets, two boys squashed behind the dresser while others feigned invisibility in the darkest corners. Gabby and as many as could jammed themselves under the bed. The measured stride of the guard came closer and Gabby fervently wished Whiteyes dusted now and again as a ball of fluff tickled his chin.

The guard stopped. Gabby heard his jacket brush the curtain. He went away.

Everyone relaxed and after a short wait straightened and unkinked themselves.

Gabby wrote a last message. "Regular meetings too dangerous. I'll give the sign for them; otherwise pass news by secret message. Get ready for hunt and cover for me when I'm gone."

One by one the boys crept away until only Gabby, Whiteyes and Beauty were left.

"I stole some cookies. Want some?" Beauty thrust a good smelling bag under Gabby's nose.

He took a handful and the three of them ate until the bag was empty. Then Beauty and Gabby headed toward their rooms.

Gabby felt the worry in his companion as they padded to the stairs and as they parted Beauty lightly touched his arm. "Hey, be careful in that old forest, eh?"

Gabby curled his lip but nodded. Then each went silently into his own part of the night.

All next day Gabby looked forward to the end of class when they were sent to their cubicles until supper. Now he knew the staff were too heat-weary to notice his absence he saw no problem in escaping to the cool comfort of the Wood. He grinned to think he was the only one to know the secret and he'd sure never tell.

It didn't make the rest of the time cooler though and the clock hands seemed dipped in treacle. He grew fractious and despite the heat gave a good roughing up to Mugger, a big fellow who hadn't gotten out of his way as quickly as he should. Soon Gabby held him in a neck lock begging for mercy and, disgusted by his lack of fight, Gabby released him. No guts any of them. He guessed maybe he was too good a fighter. Got 'em all scared. Grinning to himself he stole the kid's comic book to take into class. Probably got it in the last mail from home. Some guys always got mail and Gabby usually watched them open it to see what would be useful to him. He'd never received a letter in his life, but it didn't matter. Heck, why should Simon write anyway? Who needed it?

Four o clock came at last and the boys drifted lethargically upstairs, the staff to their own quarters. Gabby took a deep breath, made sure everyone was really gone, and charged into the glare of the sun. He squinted his eyes and his skin burned; the dust seemed too weary to stir around his feet. This time he was careful to keep the shed between himself and the school like Simon had told him. As he neared the Wood he wondered, for a second, if perhaps the beasts he had written of might really lurk there, but of course they didn't. The other sides of the forest maybe but not here. It wasn't that kind of place.

Cool greenness closed around him and a welcoming breeze dried the sweat from his body and filled him with energy. Gabby jumped a log and landed in a familiar clearing. It was as though he had entered a well-known, friendly room and a seed of happiness grew as he walked across it, careful not to harm the sprinkled flowers on which he and Simon had once rested.

He followed the suggestion of trail to a grove of giant cedars and felt like a pygmy as he looked up into their immense branches. A squirrel ran along one red limb looking a part of the tree itself and Gabby watched it jump from one to another. Seeing the boy, it stopped and leaned down, chattering. Then it leaped to another branch and back again, making more and more noise.

"I can't play with you. That tree's too tough for me to climb." Though the words were only in his head Gabby felt the squirrel understood because it quieted, sat on its haunches staring at him, then raced away leaving a sparrow to twitter in its place.

Gabby cocked his head to one side and listened, then he clapped his hands and the bird flew. Immediately Gabby wished he'd not frightened it and with a sigh turned to examine the red trunks that surrounded him. They were enormous, probably the biggest in the world, he thought and tried to reach his arms around one to measure it. His cheek rested on the bark and, nostrils full of the luxurious resinous smell. He suddenly felt very young and small, as though life were just beginning, and he was new and tender to face it. The streets were gone as though they had never been and for the first time, he wished he had someone to care about him. Someone like this tree; solid, protecting, someone he didn't have to fight. He leaned and thought of nothing.

"Tcik. Tcik."

Gabby's eyes focused on the face of a tiny shriveled man.

"Tcik. Tcik."

Round eyes stared and a tiny claw-like hand reached toward him. It was a monkey that hung by one foot and a tail from the lowest branch and releasing an arm from around the cedar Gabby reached his own hand, straining toward it. Cold fingers touched his and, unblinking, the monkey thoughtfully nibbled Gabby's fingertip. In a flash it swung away, up, up into the tree where it chattered and flung itself on to the next. Gabby ran below. For a while he kept up but then had to stop for breath. The wood wrapped him in silence.

As he listened, hoping for the monkey's return, he became aware of a low hum. He traced it to a hollow log and as he moved close a small brown and black body flew onto his hand. He slapped, crushing it to nothing. The hum ceased. There was no noise at all. Even the breeze was still, and a spooky shiver ran up Gabby's back as he waited, afraid to move.

An overhead branch creaked, and he looked up to see the monkey watching, furry hands covering its face as though in horror. Still nothing stirred and Gabby grew angry. What was the matter with everything anyway? He'd probably just scared all the bees away, that's why it was so quiet. He'd kill more of them if he had to.

He spat to one side and went to the log from which oozed a golden liquid. He dabbed with his finger, sniffed suspiciously, then touched it to his tongue. Honey, just like what came in jars! He thrust four fingers into it and then into his mouth. It was good! Eyes shut to appreciate it better, streamers soon wavered over shirt and chin. Even his thoughts were wrapped in sticky sweetness.

Zing. Something zipped past his ear. Separating sight from taste he saw a bee land on the log in front of him. Another joined it and then more. Gabby stepped back, absently licking his fingers. He didn't like the way the fuzzy insects watched him so quietly. One more taste and he'd leave.

Before he reached the honey, a buzzing cloud zoomed straight up and then downward to cover him. I'm being killed he thought and, terrified, awaited the pain; but it didn't come, only the tickle as bee's feet trod and their wings fanned. The horror seemed to last forever and then as if at a signal, the bees rose and settled back on the log.

Gabby's knees folded and he collapsed onto the ground. Carefully he opened one eye and then the other. He wasn't dead. He didn't even hurt. The tattered body of the bee he had smashed lay in front of him. Accusing. And he shuddered.

Gaining confidence, he sat up and checked himself for stings but couldn't find a mark. Then he saw the bees still crowded together, watching him and he felt the terror again. Slowly he stood up and walked backwards until trees blocked them from view, then he turned and ran. He raced along the twisty path until the shivers left him and then he ran out of relief at being alive.

Stopped by a tumbling stream Gabby flung himself onto his stomach and drank and drank. Calmed and thirst quenched he tugged off his shirt and plunged it into the water, scrubbing out the honey. Sweet waves surged to the pebbly shores and raced down stream. The shirt fought to follow but Gabby pulled it ashore and dunked his face, then his whole head. Gasping for breath he pulled back and stretched out on the ground to think over what had happened. The only conclusion he came to was that he was surely invincible. Even bees couldn't hurt him.

Water rushed and burbled beside him and light fluttered over his face. Delicate scents painted dream pictures on his mind.

A pebble rattled and Gabby opened his eyes to look into the monkey's ancient baby face. The animal was picking at the leather pouch, intent and curious. Gabby smiled, sat up, and took out the broken ends of the drumsticks to begin tapping a beat on his knee. The monkey watched for a moment but, after a quick look at Gabby's face, went back to picking at the pouch. Gabby watched the long fingers reach inside, scrabble, and come out triumphantly holding the sparkling hair. Gabby grabbed for it but his sudden lunge so startled the monkey that it let go and they both watched the shimmering thread ride upward on the wind until it was a small piece of gossamer, a whisper of light and then was gone.

Furiously disappointed Gabby raised his hand to strike but saw such regret in the brown monkey eyes his hand stopped. "Oh hell," he thought. "Oh hell!"

He looked again to where he had last seen his treasured possession and wondered if they should try to follow its direction.

The monkey ran back and forth as though urging Gabby to get started so he struggled into his not quite dry shirt, put his pouch and drumsticks in his pocket and plunged down a trail beside the stream after the scampering monkey's shadow.

A distant clangor stopped him. Like a beckoning finger the bell sought him out and the monkey came disconsolately back. Gabby sighed. We'll go tomorrow. He hoped the monkey really could read his mind as he headed toward the school.

CHAPTER XXI

"Were you in the forest again?" Beauty stood in Gabby's cubicle doorway and it struck Gabby how similar the kid's eyes were to the monkeys. "If you felt like it you could come down to the homework room and write us your adventures?"

Gabby had chosen to go to his cubicle after supper; now he couldn't help but rise to the bait and before long was downstairs surreptitiously passing notes to gang members who sat at nearby desks. He enjoyed watching their expressions as they excitedly read his made-up adventures. He almost believed them himself.

"Today I battled some crazed vicious bees for their honey. I scared them so much I got to eat all I wanted and I chased a huge hairy monster through trees until it was too tired to go any farther. I didn't kill it 'cause I want to save it for the hunt."

Notes returned with scrawled questions which Gabby answered to the best of his imagination. He wished he'd left a dab of honey on himself for evidence, but the kids seemed ready enough to believe him, all except Whiteyes who wore an exaggerated look of disbelief while he read. Gabby told himself the fink wasn't worth noticing but he got mad anyway. Not much he can do to hurt me, that's for certain, and he yawned and started up to bed.

It was his night to shower but he didn't feel like taking one after his wash in the stream that afternoon. He stood in the hall at a loss for what to do. He couldn't let his turn go to waste. Any kid would be happy to buy it but Gabby couldn't think of anything he wanted in exchange. As he pondered someone started upstairs. Oh hell, whoever it was could have it for nothing. The fat kid with slicked down hair who asked too many questions in class hove into view and Gabby beckoned to him.

The boy came gingerly, torn between fear and pride at having been noticed by The Killer's warlord. Gabby pointed toward the shower and the kid and then himself but the face in front of him remained vacant. Gabby reached into his pocket for paper and pencil but had left them downstairs so he tried to explain again. The kid just looked scared. Gabby mimed water over his head, tried every means he could think of to get his message across but the more he tried the more terrified the round face became. Exasperated, Gabby grasped the plump neck, propelled the boy toward the shower and, forcing him under it, turned the water on full blast.

"No, Gabby, no!"

Silly fool thinks he's drowning. Gabby watched the puckered red face and the hair sleeked toward sodden clothes. He left the squealing boy and went to bed.

By next day every boy knew Gabby had almost drowned someone. No one thought he shouldn't, it just added to their feeling of respect.

Gabby was pleased, it would have been bad had they found out he'd given his shower away for nothing. He must be careful about that sort of thing; just lucky the kid was so stupid. Gabby kept his eyebrows lowered in a heavy frown living up to his ferocious reputation and knowing it was another prod at Whiteyes' jealousy. That was just about the most enjoyable thing about it.

The helicopter arrived, stirring dust into a frenzy that hid it from sight. Gabby coughed as the brown cloud seethed through his window and clogged his nose. He didn't move away though, not for anything would he miss the only thing that proved the outside world still existed.

He felt as if he knew Joe and Tony. He admired the bright shirts they wore and the shaggy hair so different from that of the school staff who looked as though they must shave up the backs of their necks each morning. Tony had grown a beard and Gabby decided he'd grow one too as soon as he could.

The men handed down boxes and talked to the circle of teachers and guards who braved the sun for news. Gabby pressed his face to the bars and put his hands behind his ears so as to catch every word. Avidly he listened to game scores and then some dull political talk. He was about to relax his stretched body when the name Simon jerked him to attention.

"Yeh, the old fella broke out ten days ago. Pretended he was sick and scarpered from the san."

Gabby's heart thumped in his throat.

"I knew he'd never stick it. He hated walls." Joe spoke. "Remember how broke up he was when he left here? Worried about one of the kids. Poor bastard. I liked him."

"Maybe he's headed back if he was so keen on the place," Tony joked. "You'd all better keep your eyes open for him."

"Anyone who'd come here on purpose would have to be nuts." Warden's remark was met with laughter.

"Think he could walk a thousand miles?" asked someone.

"Maybe he'll rent a bike!"

The banter that followed was lost to Gabby who still heard the voice say, "Maybe he's headed back". Maybe he was! The more Gabby thought about it, the more he knew it was true. Simon was out there somewhere, right now coming toward him. There was no doubt at all in Gabby's mind that he'd make it and when he did the two of them could take off into the wood and live there forever, far in where they'd never hear the bell. Simon knew all about growing things so they could plant food and never worry about anything. The more he thought about it the closer it seemed until Gabby felt it might happen at any moment.

He took his bag from the corner and stuffed all his clothes in it ready to go. At this point common sense told him it would take Simon a lot more than ten days to get here. Probably months and months, so he unpacked again, all but one pair of socks and his pouch and drumsticks which he left as a promise to himself it would come true.

He bounced, whistling, downstairs. He didn't care about the heat, soon he'd never be too hot again. He gloated gleefully over the other boys dismally following the routine that never changed. He was going to be free while they probably stayed here forever.

"Hey, you two. Get out there and haul boxes."

Gabby didn't care. They wouldn't have him to boss for long and he went outside too involved with his thoughts to even be annoyed that Whiteyes was his work partner.

Sweat poured before they even got to the big crate that sent heatwaves into the sun. Gabby lifted his end wondering whether he should steal some clothes to pack for Simon. Not that they'd need many where they were going. Without warning the splintery wood wrenched from his grasp and the full weight of the box crashed onto his right instep.

"Christ, Gabby, I'm sorry." The lilt in Whiteyes' voice belied his words.

"Out of the way, boy. What happened?" A man ran toward them.

"I couldn't help it, sir." Whiteyes whined. "My hands are all sweaty and guess I just dropped my end."

Before the pain reached full force, Gabby shot him a murderous look, then he could think of nothing but the agony. For one desperate moment he was near tears but with a mighty effort he controlled them. He would rather die than cry.

I'm Clyde Barrow and a bullet got me in the foot. He gritted his teeth as hands removed his shoe and sock, and smiled weakly at the clustered boys, hoping he looked as pale as he felt. Two men gave him a fireman's lift up to his cubicle where he was left with his pain numbing in a bucket of ice water.

Alone, his head cleared and he suddenly realized what this meant to his plans. He was crippled. Maybe forever! How could he run away with Simon? How could he get to the wood to find his hair? It was as though Whiteyes had planted a bomb and blown up his hopes. It wasn't fair just when Simon was coming and everything. Desolate and angry Gabby swore he'd kill Whiteyes for this and wished at least he had the hair. Damn it all anyway.

They came to take his foot out of the bucket and bandage it and he barely flinched though it hurt like hell. Then they gave him a pill. Probably heroin, he thought as it went down. Now they've made me an addict. He fell asleep.

The first thing Gabby saw when he awoke was the monkey's eye watching him. Then he recognized it as a knothole in the wall lit by a lance of sunlight. Next he saw the white bandage, felt the ache, and then the suffocating heat of the room.

By the sounds he knew school was over and he wondered if the monkey waited for him. Brown eyes, monkey eyes waiting but I won't come. Cool breezes but I'll be hot and here. Damn. Damn. Damn. He thumped his foot on the bed and gasped at the pain. Someday, just before I leave with Simon, I'll kill Whiteyes. The promise made him feel better and he planned different ways he might do it. He must be smart though, not muck up his chances of escape.

He'd be sent away on the helicopter if he did it too soon and he had to be here when Simon arrived, then just as they were leaving... He dozed.

Distant doors slammed, voices came and went, and Gabby's stomach sent hunger signals. He hoped someone would remember to bring him supper. No one came. No one gives a shit about me. I could starve to death for all anyone cares. Jealous of me they are and scared.

"Hi, Gabby. How d'you feel?" It was Beauty with a tray and Gabby sat up, reaching eagerly for the food. He was glad his foot had such an impressive bandage as Beauty eyed it, waiting patiently while he licked the plate clean. Handing it back to the boy Gabby signaled for him to wait and wrote a note. I need a crutch.

Beauty studied it for a moment, then nodded.

Gabby wrote again. Call meeting tonight. Here.

"O.K. Gabby. Anything else? I'd better go."

Alone again Gabby began to plan. Even if he was laid up, he had to retain control or Whiteyes would use his absence to take the leadership for himself. He'd tell lies and the rest were probably stupid enough to believe them. Gabby figured there wasn't anyone he could trust, except maybe Beauty. The kid wasn't so bad really and if he gets me a crutch maybe the whole thing could be a stroke of luck. I'll be too crippled to do chores or keep up with the others and the hunt will be delayed 'til I'm well. The more he thought about it the better Gabby felt. He could stay lame until Simon arrived so he'd never have to lead the gang into the scary dark forest and run the risk of getting caught and sent away. Why, like his not talking, he could stay lame as long as he wanted and still be mobile enough to be in charge of things. His foot would be ready when he wanted it, He was tough, he'd heal fast. He whistled a tune and wished the pain would go away.

A guard helped him to the bathroom, but he had to sleep in his jeans as no one had thought to remove them before the swelling had gotten too much. Hot and uncomfortable he awaited midnight and the first creaks that meant the gang members were on their way. He motioned the first arrivals to sit on the floor and noticed Whiteyes came last. Afraid to be alone with me, he thought with pleasure.

He handed his notes to Tod who, after a smug look at Whiteyes, began to read, his voice stronger with each word. "I promote Tod to be my Runner in place of Whiteyes who screwed up my foot." Tod's voice rose with pride.

Gabby heard Whiteyes hiss and saw the colorless eyes flash for an instant before he seemed to coil down into himself. His venom could almost be smelled.

Tod read on, "If you want to hunt the forest, you'll need weapons. Monsters are huge and ferocious."

"We can steal knives from the kitchen, they don't count them like they used to," Pedro proffered.

Another voice eagerly added. "We can make sling shots."

"Something heavy on a long rope is good."

Suggestions flew from all corners. Only two voices were not heard; Beauty's because violence frightened him even though he was fascinated by it and Whiteyes because he sulked.

"Where'll we practice?" Fang's hoarse whisper had to be hushed.

131

"No practicing," Gabby wrote and Tod interrupted his own reading of the words with "Oh Gabby, we got to practice!"

Gabby wrote violently, "Would draw attention, search for weapons."

A short pause and finally everyone agreed to the wisdom of Gabby's command.

"It'll be a while yet I guess, won't it Gabby? I mean with your foot and all." Pirate didn't sound at all unhappy to think of the hunt as still far away.

Neither did anyone else though they all turned baleful looks toward Whiteyes, the cause of the postponement.

Gabby watched, satisfied with the way he'd managed things. They'd all be kept busy making their weapons while looking forward to when they could hunt. At the same time, they were angry at Whiteyes for maiming their leader. Stupid bloody Whiteyes, Gabby laughed inwardly and then realized that his head ached and he wanted to be left alone.

Almost immediately after everyone had gone Beauty returned clutching a shaggy mop. "It's your crutch," he explained. "Come on, try it."

Gabby saw that the grey wig of strings had been bundled into a wad and tied there. He put it under his arm and, with Beauty's help, struggled onto his sound leg. His lame foot throbbed but he managed a few hops before collapsing onto the bed.

"Will it work?" whispered Beauty anxiously.

Gabby nodded and sank back, eyes closed, feeling dizzy.

He must have slept because red streaked the sky when he awoke. He took the cool cloth away from his forehead and recognizing it as Beauty's favorite polka-dot handkerchief flung it into a corner. The mop would work well as a cane to get him down to breakfast. But time to get in a bit more sleep first.

CHAPTER XXII

Breakfast? Nothing was farther from Gabby's mind when the time came, but he willingly obeyed the man who told him to spend the day in bed. Pain throbbed and darted up his leg and into his head. As he rocked from side to side, he wondered why he felt so much worse and wished they'd bring him another pill.

As time wore on thoughts came to nag and fret him.

He had to get to the wood and find the hair. Over and over he saw the hair blow phantomlike farther away from him.

Time dragged. Everyone was in class. He had eaten the cereal and bread and butter Cook had brought him. He was bored. His leg ached.

Gabby listened. He was the only one upstairs. Carefully he struggled onto his good foot and clutched the crutch to him. For a moment everything went black and his foot throbbed, but it passed and he hobbled into the hall. He must find the hair or it would be lost forever. He leaned on the banister at the top of the stairs and rested his forehead on the cool wood. Where was Simon? He would surely understand why he'd had to do it. Had to be tough and badass. How many more days? Simon might be as far as the desert by now. Gabby hoped he'd stolen a fast car and had lots of water. Maybe he was even closer if it was really fast.

Gabby's head was spinning as he struggled back to his bed.

Something had changed. Sounds from the so long deadened outside jostled through his window along with a fresh gust of air. Gabby sat up; the heat spell had broken! Shouts burst from the playing field as though everyone had suddenly awakened from a long sleep. Gabby wanted to look outside but knew he couldn't make the stretch to the window on one foot so lay listening with tense concentration.

Beauty was bursting with news when he arrived with lunch. "Isn't it terrific to be cool again? They've eased up on the regulations against playing in the field after class and Whiteyes has invented a whole new game."

Gabby stiffened.

Beauty babbled on. "It's called Kill the Beast. Someone's picked to be beast and everyone else hunts him. It's sort of scary though, I hope they never choose me."

The eyes looking at Gabby were half excited, half scared reminding him of how the monkey had looked after it had let go of the hair. An anxious feeling clawed at Gabby's stomach. What if the little creature had found it and gone to another part of the wood?

Surely tomorrow he would be able to walk.

But he couldn't. He had hope until he arrived in the dining room next morning, nauseous and weak from pain.

The member of the staff they called Doc gave him a pill and soon after he'd sat down he could eat and go on to class where he amused himself by tripping people with his crutch and tapping kids on the head when teacher's back was turned. He kept hoping the foot would suddenly he completely better but whenever he tested it the pain flared.

From whispers going around the room the boys' focus seemed to be on the new game and the weapons each secretly worked on. Gabby couldn't resist the competition and, in the afternoon, he worked in an out of the way corner hunched over the beginnings of a boomerang. He'd never seen one except on T.V. but he figured he could surely make one as well as some old native.

At class' end he shoved it into a drawer and hopped and clumped his way outside, mind eagerly fixed on the waiting wood. Once on the field though he knew he could never make it across, already the pain throbbed angrily so he struggled to a bench and sat staring disconsolately at the ground.

A sound like angry birds attracted his attention and he saw the gang clustered in a squabbling group. Eventually one boy separated from them and fled at full speed past Gabby.

"I'm the beast," he gasped and disappeared around a corner of the building.

Gabby watched the hunters stand poised and eager as one of them counted. As soon as one hundred was reached they thundered in pursuit of their prey.

A few flashed grins at Gabby as they passed and then they all dashed on out of sight.

The beast burst from the other side of the school, snarling and cavorting ahead of the intent mob who yelled as they drew closer. Gabby leaned forward and wished he ran with them. The hunted one stopped his leaping and ran faster until every muscle strained for escape from the pack behind him. A scream choked from his throat as he was brought to the ground and dragged back to the starting line. He laughed nervously as everyone dropped around him in a panting heap.

Then they chose someone else.

The next two days were much the same. Each morning Gabby expected the foot to be better and suffered disappointment almost as painful as the pang when the bandage touched the floor. Each afternoon the wood drew him like a magnet, but he could get no farther than the playing field bench where he sat in frustration watching others play the monster game. Unlike the first days when everyone had clamored to be beast it was now necessary to hold a drawing. The relief of not being chosen seemed to add more excitement to the chase and Gabby saw real terror in the prey as imagination made hunter and hunted real. The beast's roars became screams and the hunter's shouts, hungry and savage.

In the next game that same boy who had just been dragged across the ground would shout with excitement as he joined in attacking another victim.

Some wouldn't play at all. Beauty always found some chore to be doing and one small kid from outside the gang broke into tears and refused to run. While Gabby watched him being beaten into action, he wondered what would happen if they ever forgot it was a game.

The men probably wouldn't notice the loss of one boy, they didn't pay them much attention now, caring only about getting through each day with the least effort and for the liquor that consoled them. Gabby stretched and, bored with the squabbling, went inside.

Next afternoon the wood's pull proved stronger than the pain in his foot and, making sure he was unnoticed, Gabby hobbled behind the shed. The distance from there seemed impossible but he made it and collapsed, gasping, into filigree shade. Pain washed from him and the everyday world disappeared.

Light and free and peaceful he watched camouflage patterns make his body and the ground one. An ant climbed to his knee without pause. Leaves fluttered and played with sun flecks and in a patch of blue a large bird soared and wheeled, sun striking russet feathers. Gabby glided with it. Wind in face. Clouds brushing wing tips. Soft.

The spicy smell of cedar called, and he crawled through a jungle of ferns to the dusky grove of big trees. A group of twittering canaries darted, like naughty boys in a cathedral, and brightened the branches with buttery dots. One sat still, puffed his chest, and burst into a clear trill. Up and down the scale it sang, then up, up the shaft of light that touched him. It was as though the sun itself sang and Gabby laughed with delight and clapped his hands to join the chorus that now filled the glade. Whirr. In one moment, they were gone. Far away another song started.

A wave of melancholy floated over Gabby as he looked inward and saw a small dirty boy run along rubbish strewn streets fighting everything and everybody, even the big loud woman who was his mother but whom he saw so seldom that when she finally went he hardly noticed. Prison hadn't been much different from the streets; same kids, same hassles. So long as he was on top everything was O.K.

Again, as though at the end of a long tunnel, Gabby saw that very small boy crying, locked in an empty room where he played with cockroaches for companionship. He'd made a pet of one and his mother came home and squashed it.

He saw himself a little older pushed into the streets where bigger boys took the few possessions he had and made sport of him until he learned to defend himself. Learned to fight and hate and be smart. He acknowledged that everything that had happened to him had been good; had made him mean and tough enough to be the Warlord he was now. Suddenly it all seemed far away and unimportant.

Gabby's drifting eyes stopped short. The great white Unicorn stood across from him between the trees.

Instantly he knew it. Recognized the glow and the sweet scent of dreams. Hadn't he carried the hair against his side for months? "When you find the animal it comes from, you'll have found something wonderful." Simon had said that and now boy and magical beast looked into each other's eyes.

The Unicorn saw a young creature so frail and lonely it made his heart ache, and Gabby saw a well of deep understanding that flooded him with feelings he had never known. Entranced he waited as the majestic creature stepped lightly toward him and he felt its breath warm and gentle on his cheek. As if on its own one of Gabby's hands lifted to the gleaming forehead from which grew the golden horn. As if in a trance he straightened the silken forelock, hand trembling. He wanted to laugh and dance and sing, but instead he stood quietly, cheeks wet with happiness.

Sudden hope sprang in Gabby's heart. Perhaps now he could stay with the Unicorn forever?

As though it read his thought the Unicorn snorted and flattened its ears from which Gabby understood he must return to the school, but he also knew that whenever he came to the wood the Unicorn would be waiting. It was as though they had struck a pact and a misty curtain had drawn aside, letting them be together.

The white muzzle touched Gabby's cheek and ghostlike the great beast melted among the trees. Gabby saw the glimmer of tail hairs, then he was alone.

He left the wood, moving in a dream, trailing his crutch through the grass behind him until he crumpled with returned pain at his first step onto the playing field. As he scrambled up, he wondered how he had managed to forget his foot completely while in that other place - but then he was starting to believe anything could happen there.

Dusk peppered the school. Gabby realized he was missing supper and that he was very hungry. Smells of meat loaf met him in the hall but he daren't go into the dining room late. Instead he struggled upstairs and lay on his bed. He felt empty and it didn't seem to be only his stomach. It was a kind of lonesome, not all there, feeling as though he had forgotten something. It made him restless and irritable. He looked under his pillow. Stupid Beauty hadn't left him anything today just when he needed it most!

Staring at the ceiling, the grain in the wood formed pork chops, legs of lamb, swirls of pudding, fruit. Gabby saw food wherever he looked.

Even the face of the guard looked like a big ham for a moment. "What are you doing here, boy? Why aren't you in the dining room?"

The guard had his hand on the butt of his gun and Gabby felt proud to be the cause of such caution.

"Well?"

Gabby pointed to his bandage and grimaced.

The guard looked doubtful. "Well don't you make a habit of sneakin' around, d'ya hear? I swear you weren't here a while back." Muttering he yanked the curtain closed and went away.

Gabby knew he was lucky it wasn't the other guard, Bob, who had found him. Since the attack on him that one was just looking for an excuse to exact revenge, preferably when no one was around.

Chairs scraping in the distance reminded Gabby that the boys were now probably getting dessert. Maybe big wobbling bowls of Jello with chunks of fruit in it - or cake.

Gabby poured a glass of water from his jug and glugged it down. He ate some tooth paste and then wished he hadn't.

After what seemed hours, he heard the sound of boys collecting their books for study. Then quiet again. He forced his thoughts away from his stomach. It really did seem that he could get away with almost anything using his foot as an excuse and acting innocent. Seemed like it worked.

"Gabby!" Beauty's timid whisper was welcome. "Are you O.K.? Got you an apple."

Is that all? You'd think he could have brought more than one measly apple! Gabby grabbed it and wrenched off a big bite, not looking up until he'd eaten the stem. Beauty had gone.

Later Tod appeared. "Hi Gabby. Need anything?"

Gabby shook his head. There was no way of getting food now and he knew Tod must have another reason for being here. He watched as he pulled something from his waistband.

He held a gleaming blade sharpened like a razor on both edges, and with a wad of cloth for a handle. Gabby inspected it with little interest although inwardly he burned with envy.

"Isn't that something, eh? I bet I could kill most anything with that." Tod tenderly ran his thumb along one edge. "When do you think we can go on the hunt? The kids are pretty eager after playing the game and all."

Gabby pointed to his foot and shrugged.

"Yeh. Maybe it'll heal fast. That Whiteyes sure slowed things up," Tod stopped and listened. Boots sounded on the stairs and he darted back to his own cubicle.

Gabby lay and thought about the steel blade, wishing it was his. Of course, it wouldn't be much good at a distance like his boomerang. He imagined his curved weapon sailing straight and true right to the head of a grizzly bear. Then he saw himself carry the bear out of the forest, boys jumping excitedly around him. He'd let Tod skin it with his knife.

That'd be good. He didn't fancy that job though he could advise how to do it. Hadn't he often inspected the skin down at Goldstein's pawn shop?

Then Gabby remembered that Tod would never use his knife, not in a hunt anyway. The kids would never have the guts to go without Gabby leading them and he and Simon would soon be far away. He wondered where Simon was now. Maybe washing in the pond everyone had swum in; maybe closer, maybe tomorrow! Gabby felt he couldn't wait a day longer. There was something else to look forward to, but he couldn't quite remember what it was. Something that made him warm inside.

A reason he didn't need the hair anymore. Damn it, why can't I remember!

Gabby dreamed he chased something through the wood. He carried a grenade and when he looked behind, he saw the rest of the gang crawl out of the sea to come after him. He just about caught up to the thing he chased and raising his arm he threw the grenade. I forgot to pull the pin was the thought in his mind as he half awoke, and though the dream ended, foreboding shadowed the rest of the night.

CHAPTER XXIII

Gangrene! They'll cut it off: Stricken with horror Gabby stared at the wizened gray black swelling of a foot from which he had just removed the bandage. The gang would never accept a one-legged warlord. How could he fight? He spread some ointment over the monstrosity and wrapped it again, fears diminishing as the strangeness disappeared from view.

Clutching his crutch, he swung along the hall and started the awkward descent of the stairs. A fly hovered in front of his nose. He tried to blow it away, but it teased and buzzed him until the landing where he could let go of the rail to swat it. Damn his foot, damn Whiteyes!

The second floor was deserted, everyone already back to afternoon class, and on a sudden notion Gabby set off toward Whiteyes' cubicle. None of the adults bothered about where he was anymore, barely able to move, lagging behind the others. Of course, he took care to look a lot lamer than he really was. It worked so well sometimes he felt almost invisible. Still the pain wasn't much fun.

One quick look around Whiteyes' room and he snatched the full water jug. As he poured it onto the middle of the bed it made a satisfying sloshing sound. Splash. Drip onto the floor below. Gabby tossed the contents of the bureau drawers into the puddle. A photo fell face up, showing a man and woman and three boys, all versions of Whiteyes. It was unbearable to think there were more like him and viciously he stabbed a hole in the face of one who leered at the camera; Poked with the end of his crutch as though he killed a live thing, until there was nothing left.

Feeling better he continued downstairs. It had been a bad day. From the start something had bugged him making him strangely anxious, dreading something but he didn't know what. He'd stubbornly refused to do any work all morning and now, carving his boomerang, his stomach buzzed like a nest of wasps. He couldn't bear sitting still and sent his weapon on a short test flight. It whanged into the wall showing not the slightest inclination to return. Disgusted Gabby left it where it fell and at that moment the bell rang, setting loose a tumult inside him. He stood in the doorway and looked toward the wood filled suddenly with a strange reluctance to go there. He hopped to an outside bench. It wobbled as Beauty sat next to him. Idly they watched the start of a game.

"Hey Gabby, you want I should get you a gun?"

"A gun?"

"I can get one easy. For the hunt."

The image caught hold. Real power. It was Gabby's dream to have a gun someday, but it had seemed a lot farther off.

"I wouldn't offer to get it for anyone else but you're special. I know where cook hides an extra one no one knows about. Even if he found out it was gone, he wouldn't say anything 'cause he's not supposed to have it. Want it?"

Gabby nodded, then gripped the boy's arm, putting a finger to his lips.

"Naw, don't worry. I won't tell no one."

The herd of hunting boys thundered past and left the two on the bench like a couple of chickens after a hurricane, thoughts scattered like feathers.

Beauty drifted away and the churning in Gabby's stomach began again as the wood sent a breeze full of promises he was afraid wouldn't come true. A deep sigh, a shrug, and he stood up. No one was around to see him begin the painful hike toward his hidden entrance and he paused on the boundary where parched ground met lush wood growth. All the turmoil he had felt during the day now rose to a peak, warning him not to risk a disappointment more than he could bear but with a defiant push of his crutch he swung into the wood.

Ah, relief from pain. He made himself look at flowers, listen to singing birds, but all the while he sought something back in the twilight of the trees.

The Unicorn! Only the unsettled cloud of mane showed he had not stood there statue-like for hours. With a gasp of relief and joy Gabby dropped his crutch and flung himself forward to hug the strong neck and press his cheek against the pulsing throat. You are real! I thought you were, perhaps, only a dream.

Together they started through the wood Gabby skipping and prancing around the Unicorn who moved in a tide of swirling fetlocks. Gabby would run ahead and tell himself that when he turned the Unicorn would be gone but always it was there, and he would run back leaping and joyful.

A spider's web hung across the path and the spider raised its front legs in salutation, then continued to spin. Knowledge seeped into Gabby's mind telling him that this web never caught flies but only drops of dew and windblown seeds for the spider's nourishment. He was about to push through when the Unicorn firmly nudged him around it and Gabby was ashamed to have almost destroyed the fragile barricade. His memory flipped quickly over other harms he had done the wood and he hoped the Unicorn didn't know.

As they travelled the trees changed. Some bore crimson flowers around where hummingbirds hovered and darted, and others had wide flat leaves where lizards scuttled. The more he looked the more life and color Gabby saw and he felt the presence of much he could never quite see however hard he peered.

The branch overhead rustled busily. Gabby grinned a welcome at the monkey who dropped to his shoulder and nibbled an ear. With a spring it was gone again, scampering high up a palm tree to return hugging a coconut which it, chattering with glee, held out to Gabby. Gabby had seen coconuts on store shelves but didn't know what was inside and turned it wondering what to do next. Again, the monkey rushed off returning this time followed by a large black bird with a sharp rainbow-colored bill. It fluttered to the nut Gabby had set down and stabbed the indentations on top until there was a good hole. Again, the nut was given to Gabby who tipped it and poured tepid liquid into his mouth. It tasted horrible and he was just about to spit in disgust when he noticed the monkey's look of eager expectancy, and the bird who watched him with head to one side. Gabby swallowed and took another gulp. It tasted better, and then quite good. Sweet and refreshing it poured down his throat and when it was all gone, he licked his lips while monkey and bird cavorted joyfully around him.

They split the nut into a pile of satiny pieces and began to eat. Mouth full Gabby looked up and was engulfed by sheer happiness which sent him running to the Unicorn who had stood to the side watching. He pushed his forehead into the solid shoulder and twisted the familiar mane tight around his fists.

The monkey joined them and, leaving the bird to finish the coconut, the three rambled on. Gabby was unable to restrain from skipping and hopping as they went.

The wood became more open and blueberries and fat red huckleberries kept Gabby's hands and mouth so busy he scarcely noticed an increasing roar until they rounded a boulder and were enveloped in the thunder and swirling mist of a waterfall that plunged deep into a turbulent pool. The Unicorn dipped its muzzle among the wavelets, the reflection of its horn powdered gold across the surface, breaking and reforming in a magical column.

Gabby fell to his stomach alongside and sucked up water that tasted of mountain peaks and the sky above the rainbow. He drank in feelings beyond all space and time until he could drink no more and pulled back to look at himself. In the moving water two unfamiliar dark eyes full of sunshine laughed back at him.

A tug at his foot brought his attention to the monkey who was struggling to remove the dirty bandage. It did look ugly and Gabby unwound it, wondering again how he had so easily forgotten the pain. Air fanned the swelling and after removing his other sneaker Gabby plunged both feet into the pool and felt the current whirl past, tickling and caressing the damage from his bones. The monkey played with the bandage, first washing, then waving it like a streamer over its head while Gabby watched, half dozing in the roar of the falls.

Shadows grew long. It was time to go. Gabby drew his feet from the water that slid from them in a solid shining rush. Swoosh. He did it again. Swoosh. Side by side on the bank he could see no difference between them. No bruises. No swelling. No pain.

He stood up and stretched. Each muscle and cell tingled with such well-being that he sprang into a cartwheel and with a bound was among the trees running as fast as he could. Like a ghost, the Unicorn ran alongside. Gabby flung his head back and laughed as they sped through branches that never slapped and jumped logs that never tripped. He could feel other animals running too, sharing his wild joy although he couldn't see them, and the only sound was as if a boisterous wind rushed and swept through the foliage. Gabby wanted to run forever, but the Unicorn blocked his way and with a firm snort nudged him in the direction of the school then, without waiting, was off in a haze of mane, tail and flying hooves. Gabby rushed to catch up and soon they raced side by side to where the trees ended and Gabby leaned, laughing and breathless, against the shining shoulder.

The monkey dropped from a tree with the bandage which Gabby refused to accept although the monkey clucked anxiously, insisting. Gabby refused to take it until the Unicorn gave him a stern look, then, with a shrug, Gabby began to re-bind his now flawless foot, remembering how necessary it was for him to appear lame in that other world. Gratefully he stroked the monkey's soft head. It held his hand against its cheek for an instant then darted behind a bush to return with the crutch.

Gabby was ready to leave and with a sigh he stepped across the boundary. Instantly pain slashed his foot and the wood disappeared as though a fog lowered, blotting his memory.

The line was already formed for supper when Gabby hobbled into place.

"You silly little faggot. I know it was you tore up my room. Always skulking about!"

He turned to see Whiteyes towering angrily over Beauty.

"Honest I didn't!" Beauty's protests went unheard and his face became purple as Whiteyes pulled his collar tight.

"Just 'cause you dig Gabby. You rotten pervert you!"

The others shuffled impatiently.

"Come on!"

"Move it!"

"Fight somewhere else, we're hungry!"

The struggling boys were pushed along and finally separated.

Gabby was amused and somewhat surprised that Whiteyes didn't know it was he who had ransacked his cubicle. *Figures I'm too lame to go anywhere. Guess they all think I'm too crippled to do much. That's good.* Gabby sat down and looked across the room to where Beauty nervously played with his knife and fork. *He won't mind taking the blame for me. Do him good.*

CHAPTER XXIV

Gabby walked with his hand on the Unicorn's shoulder and watched the mane float and settle with each stride. Green shadows speckled them, and the breeze blew fresh and clean. Four afternoons now they had spent together, and each time Gabby learned something new and each time he tried to hold onto his memories when he left but always they faded like morning mist.

They hadn't gone far this day when they stopped at the entrance to a leaf canopied glade. Gabby drew back against the Unicorn when he saw the enormous leopard who lay watching three tumbling cubs through half closed eyes. She thumped her tail slowly on the daisy covered turf and purred a loud welcome as her eyes inspected Gabby for a moment, then turned back to her youngsters.

Gabby's fears dissolved in the face of such soft cat beauty and when the Unicorn gave him a push with its nose he went eagerly to the cubs and knelt beside them on the ground. They clambered over his knees, patted his chin with plump paws; then tumbled head over heels to the ground. Gabby laughed out loud. Out loud! He stopped, surprised. I have a voice, he thought. I have a voice!

And he laughed again, rolling the cubs onto their backs, fuzzy bellies writhing to be upright. They raced around the glade, ears flat, spines arched, and tails hooked high. Back to tumble again with Gabby rolling with them, a cub himself, until played out they sprawled to rest.

The clearing rumbled to contented purrs and the sun glinted along the coils of the watching Unicorn's horn. Gabby gave a farewell stroke to three sleepy foreheads and joined his friend to stroll along the soft trail. He couldn't stay sedate for long; everything was too wonderfully exciting, and he bubbled inside like a kettle. He swung on a vine and did a cartwheel, then hopped back to the Unicorn on one leg. As he came close the Unicorn arched its neck and wheeled away with a high whinny and Gabby ran after it until the Unicorn reared, spinning toward him and Gabby darted from under the flashing hooves to rear himself and gallop in imitation. Retreating, advancing, plunging and snorting the two played, and the wood rang with their game.

Stepping high on springs they approached each other. Almost touching, they spun around: each at the same instant and Gabby collapsed laughing onto the grass. The Unicorn also lay down and Gabby shuffled so as to lie his head on the spot where neck met warm shoulder blade. A tiger prowled by, then a giraffe and stranger animals Gabby didn't recognize. They all looked at him with friendly eyes and he knew the wood was his home.

But still he had to leave it and circling back to where he had left his crutch Gabby and the Unicorn were alone again. A raucous noise startled them and pushing branches aside they looked onto the playing field where a group of boys carried a smaller one by his arms and legs. His nose bled a dark stream across his face and his tormentors chanted, "Kill the creature! Kill the beast!"

Gabby shuddered, clutched by a strange panic, and he flung his arms around the Unicorn's neck, clinging tightly, and afraid. Slowly they went to where he could leave unobserved and when he looked back Gabby saw only trees although he imagined a gentle whinny floated to him through the still air.

Hobbling from behind the shed he found himself close to the churning mass of boys and eagerly he hurried closer. A pungent smell reminded him of the night they battled the guard and it sent chills up his spine.

Panting, glittery eyed hunters surrounded him.

"Hey Gabby, you should have seen. That was one hell of a game!"

You should have seen this monster fight when we caught him," Fang gave the leg he held a shake. "Shall we let him go now, Whitey?"

The victim was dropped, and the gang gathered around Gabby. "Is your foot almost better? Whiteyes says we can go on the real hunt soon."

Gabby smiled and nodded, then frowned, miming patience until his injury was healed. After that he made a great show of struggling painfully upstairs.

Day followed day and boy and Unicorn became a familiar sight to the wood creatures. Gabby was accepted as a delicate orphan fawn would be and the animals played with him as with their own.

Gabby rubbed his face in the fur of a polar bear and raced a young gazelle. He explored the den occupied by a family of red foxes and was lifted high by the rough trunk of an elephant to ride on its back. He climbed trees with the monkey and sat in the coils of a python. But never did he stray far from the Unicorn who always made sure he left the wood in time although it became harder each day.

It was as though Gabby were two boys. One who laughed and belonged to the wood and the other silent Warlord of the Killers and they never mingled.

Autumn brought gusty winds that scudded clouds across the sky before they could empty their full loads. The gang became restive and pressed Gabby again into writing of the creatures they soon hoped to hunt. His imagination boiled in the cold homework room and spilled out made up scenarios of what might be in the Dark forest. All ugly, vicious, boy hungry monsters.

In the night meetings the gang listened as Whiteyes read what had been written earlier, packed close, eyes alight and Gabby shared the excitement with them.

Sometimes when he was neither awake nor asleep, he heard animal calls from the wood and his two selves would collide in confusion so he would awaken with a cry and lie hoping no one had heard.

The night of the first frost he tossed and whimpered under the knives poised over his head. He fought to escape, to open his eyes, and when they did, he looked into the muzzle of a gun.

"Do you like it Gabby? It's all loaded and ready to fire."

It took a few moments for the voice to make sense through his shock but slowly Gabby recognized Beauty's timorous whisper. "It's got six shots in it. I couldn't get any more. He keeps the ammo locked up. It's good though, eh Gabby? Isn't it?"

Gabby took the cold metal into his hand. He had never held a gun before and it felt stern and solid. It made him feel strong and powerful.

"When you want to fire you just pull back the top and it chambers a shell. It can't shoot 'til you do that."

Gabby pushed Beauty away and squinted along the barrel, aiming around the room. His hand shook from the weight of it and he sniffed the muzzle like he'd seen them do in movies.

He looked up at Beauty and signaled for secrecy.

"I sure won't tell no one, Gabby. You can count on me. You do like it don't you?"

A floorboard creaked in the corridor and both boys sprang to the curtain and looked out. Gabby thought he saw a shadow move at the head of the stairs, but he wasn't sure. Nothing stirred, though they waited until they could bear it no longer and Beauty slipped away leaving Gabby to gloat over his new possession. He stroked the blue metal and turned it over, his emotions a mixture of enormous pride and disquiet. The thrill of ownership grew and with it the fear of loss. Kneeling half under his bed he pried up the board, threw the ointment out from the cavity and carefully laid the gun in its place. It fit perfectly. Quickly Gabby darted to his door and checked to make sure no one was about then he again knelt by the gun which lay as though in a coffin. He had never owned anything so wonderful and he picked it up again. At last he set it back in its hiding place and lowered the board.

At that moment something clattered beside him, and the shock made him hit his head a noisy bang on the bed frame before he scrambled on top to feign sleep under his blanket.

While the enquiring step of the guard came closer Gabby wondered if his head was bleeding, soaking the bed, a dead giveaway. Light reddened his eyelids and he felt himself being looked at, sensed the presence come close to the bed, smelled the man's hair cream and whiskey breath as he bent down toward the gun. Something thudded onto the foot of the bed and the guard left.

Gabby lay dead still except for his fingers which felt for the object. He grasped it and recognized the tube of ointment, his breath whistling out in relief.

Next day at lunch Beauty appeared with a black eye and bruises over the rest of his face. Probably got caught swiping something, Gabby thought and planned to find out later- but he forgot all about it.

CHAPTER XXV

Steady relentless rain changed the playing field into a quagmire over-night.

They must have picked this place for its lousy weather, Gabby thought as he looked out at it and wondered how difficult escaping to the Wood might be now everyone was shut inside. He shivered and sniffed the mold that already seemed to permeate the building. Bloody place! They could at least have put in some heating when they built it.

Bed covers were dank and cold, and boys slept fully dressed, curled into tight balls. Within two days most had the beginnings of a cold and soon everyone lived in his own stuffed up world. Contrary to his expectations, Gabby, who seemed immune to illness, now found himself even freer than before.

Rain drenched him each day as he darted through it but once in the Wood's eternal Spring he dried and ran to find the Unicorn who whinnied a welcome and allowed Gabby to ride on its broad back. The monkey, usually nearby, would swing from a branch onto Gabby's shoulder.

Some afternoons they just wandered peacefully nibbling ripe fruit and sniffing good smells; other times Gabby would dismount to run and play chase, all kinds of animals joining in. But best was when they all settled to rest and Gabby lay propped against the flank of the dozing Unicorn watching colors flit from hair to hair through the horse like creature's coat and across the silken eyelashes. At times as he ran his fingers through the restless mane Gabby realized perfect happiness that filled him to bursting, but then behind it always lurked a shadow he didn't understand, and a hint of fear would seep into his day.

Back in school colds were diagnosed as flu and teachers became too ill to teach. There was little attention to spare for the few boys still up and Gabby was able to spend more time with the Unicorn. No one noticed his absences, so often he stayed out until after supper. The Wood was his world and time in school was just a boring necessity. Damp and cold, with almost everyone in bed, the building felt deserted and Gabby suffered the boredom of nothing to do but the chores left undone by all who were sick.

In the Wood it was just the opposite, time flew and there was too much to do. He could now climb trees almost as nimbly as the monkey, he crept through undergrowth as silently as the softly padding cats, and above all he learned to be gentle. Now his fingers could walk the surface of the pond as lightly as a skeeter's feet. He even knew how not to take too much honey from the bees who buzzed cheerfully around him as he ate.

But the most amazing thing he learned was to laugh, something people seldom did in his world. A snicker sometimes or the kind that made someone else feel bad. Not deep wholehearted laughter that even the perpetrator joined. The animals did such funny things and one day when Gabby met a sloth hanging upside down and when it opened one sleepy eye and winked at him something bubbled up inside him and burst out in laughter he couldn't stop. Tears poured down his cheeks until he had trouble staying upright and the whole wood and its creatures seemed to join his mirth. Even the Unicorn lifted its upper lip, snorted and stamped its foot while the monkey sat on its back with his hands pressed over his mouth and eyes sparkling. What a wonderful feeling! From then on laughter was always close while in the wood.

But outside it was nonexistent. Life in the Mystical wood was only a dream inhabited by a different boy. Gabby knew that in real life, to survive, he must bury all those soft feelings he had so lately discovered.

Suddenly the flu bug was gone and things back to normal locking Gabby again into long hours of classes. A teacher thought to look at his foot and finding it better took away his bandage and his excuse to be lame. The boys saw and grinned expectantly.

Word went out that a meeting would be held at Whiteyes' that night. Gabby wondered why it was changed from his cubicle where it had been held since his accident. It bothered him for a moment but then he decided it was just as well, it always made him edgy to know someone sat right on top of his gun anyway. He hadn't thought much about the gang lately, he'd better keep a watch on things. His eyes roamed to the wood and he wished Simon would hurry.

Phew! The sickening stench that met Gabby the moment he entered Whiteyes' cubicle made him gag. The other boys shuffled in similar discomfort and pulled protective shirts over their noses. The meeting began immediately or Whiteyes would most surely have lost his audience.

Like a magician performing a trick Whiteyes opened his top drawer and took out a small bundle which he placed with exaggerated care in the middle of the bed. With a flourish he flipped aside the edges of material and everyone gasped and drew back as the putrid odor almost suffocated them.

"It does smell pretty rank, but it's been in my drawer since yesterday," Whiteyes apologized. "Come and look!"

Noses tightly pinned, the boys edged closer and Gabby made out a handkerchief covered by dark splotches with a darker blob in the middle. He turned away for a breath and when he looked again saw a tiny dead bird with a shattered head. For a second there was a painful flutter in his chest and an ache in his throat, but he smothered it with congratulatory slaps on his second-in command's back.

"I killed it with this." Whiteyes proudly held up a slingshot. "No one saw me. It was sitting on a tree stump and I just happened to have this in my hand. Only one shot too."

Excitedly everyone strained to see; it was the excitement of hounds at their first scent of blood.

Faces turned toward Gabby. "Let's go Gabby. We're all ready and your foot's okay now."

His gang awaited his answer, spearing him with their eagerness.

"Our weapons are made and it's cool."

It was already decided. There was no reason not to go. Their excitement caught hold of Gabby and grew. A real hunt like in the movies. It might be fun. They wouldn't get caught if they were careful. It was kind of good to see them all looking and waiting for his words and Gabby took out his pad importantly and wrote. "Next full moon."

"We just had one. It's got to be sooner."

The faces again waited and Gabby, spurred by their impatience, wrote and handed it to Whiteyes who read aloud, "Thursday night. The helicopter comes that day. Guards will be drunk.'"

"Hey good thought, Gabby!"

Grunts of agreement and anticipation exploded from the gang. They all knew about the bottles that arrived in each cargo and recognized the red eyes and short tempers of their keepers the next day.

A shiver of doubt chilled Gabby. He had only two days to explore the black part of the forest he was supposed to have been visiting all this time. What if there were awful animals like those he'd written about? Then again, what if there weren't?

He didn't sleep well that night and for the first time dreaded the bell that signaled the end of afternoon school next day. When the time did come, he went outside, looked longingly in direction of the Wood, then started the opposite way.

"Hey you. Where d'you think you're going?"

Half relieved to be stopped Gabby turned toward the guard called Bob, the scratches still livid on his face. He saw the recognition in his eyes and saw the lips curl in a snarl. "Get upstairs and bring down your laundry, Boy!"

Gabby remembered the dirty clothes he had stuffed in his bottom drawer and hated the man for snooping around his room. Slowly he returned to the building and, as he passed, the guard gave him a shove, "Dirty bastard," he muttered.

Gabby gave him the "look" and went upstairs.

The gray bundle sank soggily in the tub of water and Gabby swished it around a few times. Now he was stuck here in the laundry room he wanted to be outside doing what had to be done. If the hunt wasn't successful, he'd be in trouble. He had to get going! Urgency galvanized him into action and he splashed the clothes, squeezed and had them hung on the line in no time.

At least the chore had got him officially outside. After checking to make sure no guards were in sight, and before he could think twice, he ran full speed into the forest.

It was dark here. And quiet. A dead, listening kind of quiet. Maybe I can pretend I've been here and not go any farther, he thought, but then he imagined Whiteyes' jeering face and clenched his fists. He'd show that jerk! With determination he pushed through while brambles tore his clothes and raked his bare arms. He was sweaty and bleeding when he got through and stood on bare hard ground beneath trees that completely blocked the sky and closed a wall around him. Gabby breathed hard. He knew things hid behind them, watching and ready to pounce. Nothing moved and the only sound was a steady drip that grew louder the longer he listened. A groan made the hairs on his neck rise and he couldn't have moved if he'd wanted to.

Caw! Caw! A crow flapped and yammered above him, snapping Gabby's head back in shock. Seeing the familiar bird released him and he gave himself permission to leave. Surely there were plenty of monsters here, no need to look farther. He forced himself to stay at a steady walk. When he stumbled over a log he couldn't remember seeing before and a branch snapped, he almost broke his intention not to run, but he didn't. Mud oozed over his sneakers and before he knew it, he stood ankle deep in a bog. Brackish water rose to the top of his socks and he was sure snakes writhed just beneath the surface. Around him the forest grew darker. Gabby ran. Mud splashed and branches whipped as he tore through them blindly. He felt the hot breath of something chasing him, and then he burst onto the playing field and heard the usual sounds of boys playing.

He looked at the forest behind him and nothing stirred. He'd been a fool. He saw the mess he was in and tearing off some leaves wiped away the blood and mud, angry at himself for being scared. "Killers" were never scared. Especially their leader.

He strolled toward the building and from the corner of his eye saw Whiteyes look up from where he twisted the arm of a smaller boy. He began to run toward Gabby who ignored him until a freckle covered arm nudged his obnoxiously and Whiteyes' whiney voice spoke in his ear. "Been getting things ready for the hunt? It'd better be a good one. You and your beasts. Ha! Those dumb clucks believed your lies but I'm not so stupid. Bet you'd be scared if you saw something bigger than a caterpillar!"

Gabby lunged at him but Whiteyes had already bolted and before he could give chase a voice interrupted.

"Come here, Boy."

Gabby turned with insolent slowness toward the guard.

"Your foot seems so good now I'll have to see you're put back on the tougher chores. Now get the hell inside and clean up. Your clothes look like a pig's been wearing them! Everything clean, you hear boy? Clean!"

Gabby started up the steps. He hardly thought about the guard, his mind was too crowded with anger toward Whiteyes and his undermining of Gabby's authority. He wondered if he should wait until Simon came to get rid of him. He must though. It would ruin everything if he lost his temper and killed the jerk too soon. He thought about how scared the others would be when he took them into the forest and the more he thought about it the more he appreciated how brave he was to have gone there alone. They'd all realize that. Anyway, he would take his penknife next time.

Gabby showered in his clothes, adding bog water to the drain's swirl and as he watched it, he relived his adventure in the Forest and heard Whiteyes' voice saying, "But where are the vicious animals? What's to be scared of? Big deal! We saw all this in the crappy old bus coming here."

And he'd be right, Gabby thought as he watched the last muddy stream gurgle away. He had to go back and find something really scary.

The next day played at Indian summer, fooling birds so they rushed about with bits of nesting material. Gabby did not look forward to this afternoon's return to the forest, A night's sleep and the sun had dispelled his fears, but he was missing the Unicorn and there wasn't time to visit both places.

When the hour came for his absence to go unnoticed, he chose a better way into the waiting darkness and instead of having to struggle through brambles he entered at once the dead, fusty gloom of big trees. Today nothing could spook him. He was an Indian. A thorn punctured his finger. He sucked the blood and put a smudge on his forehead as war paint. He could have wished for more light, but he could see alright and he knew it was only branches rubbing that made that moaning sound. With his penknife he cut slashes on the trees to mark his path and enjoyed marring their threatening hugeness. He swung all around one massive trunk just to prove there was nothing there.

A squeal came from behind a clump of bushes. Creeping stealthily Gabby saw five rabbits nervously sniffing the air. One thumped and they all took off, wild and raggedy looking. They were different from the fat, playful ones who were Gabby's friends in the Wood, or the white ones Simon had brought. He quickly brushed them from his mind now, pulled a branch to its limit and let it snap behind him.

This place was so different from his own wood which he hadn't been able to visit for days. What if the Unicorn thought he was never coming back, and it and the monkey went away so he could never find them again? That wouldn't happen though. Gabby stifled the spark of panic. The Unicorn would know he just couldn't get there. It would wait for him. Tomorrow he'd go "home." Use of that word thrilled Gabby and he said it to himself again and wished he could say it aloud. Why not? But no, this wasn't the time, he must keep quiet and get this job done. It would take something bigger than rabbits to thrill the Killers.

Gabby found his way blocked by a giant fallen tree. He clambered onto the trunk which he balanced along to where the roots clawed grotesquely toward hidden sky. He peered inside their tangle. It seemed just the place for a monster to live and sure enough Gabby saw a big hole and tracks leading into it. Mustering all his courage he scrambled closer and peered in. Blackness and a musty smell met him and built the shape of a fearsome monster in his mind.

That was good enough; it was all he needed and thankfully he backed away. When he was a safe distance, he made sure he could find the place again and, following the marked trees, walked boldly, exultation welling in him. The boys with all their weapons would have a great hunt after whatever lived in that hole and anything else they scared out of hiding. Gabby caught his foot in a vine and sprawled full length on the ground. He ripped it in half and flung the end against a tree with a resounding slap. Stupid thing wouldn't trip him again!

He stepped calmly into the final glimmers of sunlight just as the supper bell sounded.

The short final meeting that night before the hunt brought disappointment to Gabby.

"We all decided it would be better to hunt during games time instead of at night," It was Whiteyes who spoke and if the others hadn't been nodding agreement Gabby would have stopped him right there. "The staff will all be drinking anyway."

Gabby had planned on visiting the Unicorn during that time and besides, the hunt would be much scarier in the dark. Shaking his head in violent disagreement he wrote frantically. "Animals not out till night. Guards won't be drunk enough." But as he heard his notes read, he knew the boys had made up their minds. The air was taut with their stubbornness.

"They're scared." Gabby recognized Beauty's whisper in his ear. "They're not brave like you. They're scared of the dark, and the animals, but they won't admit it."

Pride straightened Gabby's back and scorn curled his lip. He shrugged and agreed to their change in time but let them know he despised them for it and also that they mustn't expect as good a hunt now. Gabby left for his cubicle looking forward to the excitement ahead. After all, one more day of not visiting the wood wouldn't really matter, would it?

CHAPTER XXVI

B
ut it did matter. As soon as Gabby tugged the blanket over his nose, he knew it mattered terribly. Damn cowardly kids! Night sounds drifted through his broken window and he jumped up on his bed and looked to where the wood waited, bathed in its own mysterious moonlight. For a moment he thought he saw the luminescent glow of the Unicorn, and suddenly it was imperative that he go.

Quick as the thought he dressed and crept along the hall and downstairs. In another moment he was outside, racing across open ground to leap joyously into soft grass. The Unicorn galloped, whinnying, to meet him and Gabby hugged its neck as though he'd been away for a long, long time. The monkey sprang to its place on Gabby's shoulder and the three of them set off. The wood was excitingly different at night and Gabby met animals he had never seen before. A kinkajou popped a grape absent mindedly into its mouth while it looked at him with huge unblinking eyes and an owl flapped big soft strokes overhead, to-whooing into the distance.

At the edge of a large moon washed clearing they stopped. Gabby stood by the Unicorn's shining head, wisps of mane soft against his cheek. Their breath made silver ribbons and Gabby decided the Unicorn must be part of the moon itself it shone so brightly. The slender ears flicked, and Gabby looked to where they pointed. The ground rose, forming a small hillock upon which a pack of wolves stood silhouetted starkly against the sky. They raised their muzzles and began to howl. Softly at first, then gaining power until the sound reached right down inside Gabby, tingling his feet and pulling at his heart. Hardly knowing what he did he trotted across the moonlit space and pressed among the shaggy bodies, feeling a howl fight in his own chest. The warmth of quivering hides crowded against his legs and his soul thrilled to the wildness of the song around him. For a time, Gabby forgot he was a boy; then suddenly the howling stopped, wolves dissolved into the dark like shadows, leaving Gabby alone under the stars.

He ran back to the Unicorn and sat between its hooves, feeling soft lips muzzle his hair. Quietly the night held them in its hand.

When the Unicorn awoke him, dawn scratched the darkness and Gabby knew he must get back to the school quickly. One hand on the Unicorn's withers they trotted through the sleeping wood and together stood looking out into the world with no moon. A cuckoo called behind them and Gabby ran across the black void into the building and up to his cubicle. He had just settled into bed when the wake-up bell rang.

Excitement arced through the building so even those who knew nothing of the hunt felt something special was about to happen. The staff put it down to the helicopter's arrival and sent the boys upstairs after lunch to get rid of the nuisance of them.

Gabby sat cross legged on his bed listening to the helicopter's arrival and then the unloading of cargo. He listened to what was said but there was no word of Simon. At least they hadn't caught him, they would have mentioned that. Gabby grew bored of the long conversation about some war or other and then he shot to alertness. The pilot was speaking, Gabby recognized the little cough that punctuated the man's growly voice. "Heard these kids' time's 'bout up. Back on the streets soon I guess."

Ice swept through Gabby's veins. He'd never thought of that. It was him escaping with Simon into the Wood he saw as his future not back to the old cold life of before. Where are you Simon! He checked the corridor. Finding it empty he lifted the floorboard and took out his gun. It felt big and awkward.

He stuffed it into the waist of his jeans and then up the front of the sweater he'd been issued when the cooler weather started. Shit! It didn't fit anywhere. Even if he strapped it to his ribs where he used to carry his drumsticks it made his arm stick out at a weird angle. He stared at the unconcerned metal, disappointed. He'd sure looked forward to carrying it on this hunt and awing the rest of the gang. He'd just have to wait till they went at night when it wouldn't be necessary to hide it through classes like today. Sadly, he polished the barrel with his shirt tail and replaced it under the bed. Now he had no weapon at all. Well, hadn't his hands and feet always been enough? Besides they'd think him pretty cool to brave the forest unarmed. He was tough.

The gang's excitement blended with that of received mail and new supplies, otherwise someone would surely have noticed the eyes that continually darted to the clock and the strange bulges that distorted pockets and belt lines. Game time was met with a stampede to the field. Drunken laughter already echoed from the adult's common room. They would no longer be aware of anything their charges did.

Gabby pointed out the lightening scarred oak under which the gang members would meet, then he kicked the ball and with a yell the game began. Within five minutes Gabby waited alone, scuffing the moldy ground of the forest. One at a time the others arrived, their eyes bright with anticipation. The last to appear was Whiteyes, paler even than usual and for once he had nothing to say. Gabby gave a careless wave for them to follow and started briskly along the marked path only he could see. Jostling each other, afraid to be left, the group ran to keep up, heads nervously spinning to right and left. Gabby glanced over his shoulder and grinned to see their eager faces. They're just a bunch of sheep, he thought, I could lead them anywhere.

Snap, crunch, thud went their feet, seeming louder all the time.

Gabby stopped short causing his followers to carom into a startled heap. "Shh!" he hissed and demonstrated how to walk with flat, careful feet.

Again, they set off, quietly this time and instead of footsteps Gabby heard the snatch and rip of brambles and curses as a branch slapped from one boy to the next. It wasn't far to the log now and Gabby signaled them to get ready.

"Are the beasts near?" Pirate whispered.

"Bet there aren't any," muttered Whiteyes glancing over his shoulder.

Uneasily the boys pulled knives, slingshots and clubs from their clothes. Gabby thought of the sensation it would cause if he could only produce his gun now. Next time.

The crow flapped and cawed and Gabby laughed to see the others cower and Whiteyes push a smaller boy in front of him. He strode on leaving them to catch up in a terrified gallop. Yesterday he had been glad not to meet any ferocious animals but today he was ready for anything. Would welcome them in fact. He heard whispering and imagined Whiteyes spreading doubts. If only something would jump out on him!

As they approached the fallen tree Gabby raised a hand for caution. At that moment a grey squirrel ran, flirting along the trunk and with a yell the boys took after it. Gabby watched, unable to stop them.

He saw the surprised squirrel leap from the log and dash across the ground, missing trees it could have climbed. Close behind, the boys collided, tripping each other up in their excitement, dropping the stones for their slingshots and falling over their sharpened sticks. Before they knew it, they stood waist high in scratchy green bushes and the squirrel scolded from a high branch.

An arrow rose feebly and fell back onto Fang's head.

Cursing, he turned on the boy who held the bow beating him with the handle of his slingshot. It was starting to turn into a free for all and Gabby ran to join in, planning to get off a few good punches at Whiteyes while he had the chance.

Everything stopped. Threats and swearing turned to puzzled exclamations.

"What the hell!"

"Something itches."

"Me too!"

"Stinging nettles! Get out of these bushes everyone. I heard about them."

The boys fought their way out of the greenery onto bare ground and ended up squirming and scratching in front of Gabby.

"Why didn't you warn us, Gabby?" Whiteyes said accusingly to their leader.

Gabby shrugged. How could he know every bush in the forest? Hadn't he tried to stop them? He fought not to scratch himself. They'd see no bushes could hurt him. Luckily the rash didn't show on his dark skin and he stood to one side with what he hoped was a condescending expression while the rest jumped around and itched. He hoped they didn't see how his eyes watered from the prickling on his own arms and legs.

"Let's go. I've had enough of this." Whiteyes stamped away and the others followed. "It's a crummy old place anyway."

Concerned only with their itching Gabby was forgotten and he watched them go, hating Whiteyes until he could taste it. He stayed tense, listening, relaxing only when he heard muffled curses and splashing. Then he smiled. Angry voices slowly grew closer and disconsolate boys straggled back to him, Whiteyes sullen and angry eyed in the rear.

They crowded around Gabby. "Take us out of here will you, Gabby? There's a rotten bog back there."

Gabby just leaned against a tree and looked at them for a while. Then with a sneer and a shrug he led them out to join the faltering game in the playing field. He left the forest last, remaining behind for two minutes of delicious scratching.

By the time he joined them, those who had been left already bombarded the little band of hunters with questions. Suddenly, the center of such eager and envious curiosity, each boy swelled with importance and, nettles forgotten, they told how fearsome the forest was with trees that attacked with sword-like limbs. They talked of quicksand and the monster they chased, which bore no resemblance to the small frightened squirrel of reality. Believing their own stories, they realized how brave they were. How superior the members of the Killers were.

As their leader, Gabby received the glory and was relieved at the way things had turned out. Several times Whiteyes brought up the subject of nettles but was quickly hushed to skulk morosely in the background.

Next afternoon Gabby was free to escape for a wild galloping game with the Unicorn and a chase through tree branches after the monkey. Then he lay on his back tracing the colors in the wing of a butterfly that had settled on his knee.

At the Killer's next meeting stinging nettles were forgotten with only the thrill of adulation remaining. Everyone clamored for more.

"I'll take you if Gabby won't." Whiteyes blurted. "Maybe something scared him in there."

"Great! We're tough. We wanna go!" Everyone was looking at Whiteyes, faces eager, Gabby forgotten.

Rage rose in Gabby's gut. Had he been blinded by the magic of the Wood. He had been mesmerized by feelings that made him forget the real world where he had to be sharp to keep the power he had longed for for so long and finally achieved. He was the mean and tough Warlord of the killers and would stay that way. He gave a jab to Whiteyes' ribs knocking him half off the bed where he sat.

Gabby promised them Friday, a full week since the last.

Where the hell was Simon? If he didn't hurry, he'd ruin everything. Gabby felt bitter, things seemed to be getting out of control, his plans not quite so clear cut as before.

That afternoon as he rushed from the workshop the teacher blocked his exit. "Hey Arthur, where's the fire? Your day to clean up in here, remember? Better keep track or you'll get double duties."

Looking at the Wood beyond the man's arm Gabby almost charged through but with a surge of despair turned back. He kicked a table leg and didn't care how much it hurt his foot.

The workshop was the worst room to clean at any time with all the benches and tables, and sawdust everywhere. Today with the instructor watching it was a nightmare and left no way to get by with the usual dabs and sweeping stuff into corners. Gabby hated the smell of water on the floor.

That night Gabby stood with his chin on the windowsill and watched a slim moon rise behind the wood's leafy silhouette. He imagined sleepy eyes opening, and yawning night creatures tumbling out to play. He longed to run barefoot through silver grass and to climb silver trees, but when he crept to the stair head there was no chance of getting past the guards who played cards at the bottom.

Returned to his window Gabby listened to distant howling and remembered wolf faces turned to the stars, felt cozy shagginess against his legs. Soon as Simon came the two of them could disappear in there forever. But a sudden thought staggered him. What if Simon was mad and didn't want anything to do with him after what he'd done to the rabbits? Then what if the old guy told the Unicorn! What if it spread through the wood and they all hated him! Panic sawed like a knife. You couldn't trust adults. Had he forgotten that truth learned so young?

At that moment a white glow appeared at the edge of the trees and the harder he looked the clearer Gabby saw until he gazed deep into the great kind Unicorn eyes. It was like floating in the trough of a wave, gently easing pain and worry away. He slept.

CHAPTER XXVII

Autumn hurled gusty breaths around the school, whirling crisp leaves against windows and causing rattles in unseen corners. Boys' minds were as empty and wayward as the wind and math and science slid over them barely touching, through long fidgety hours.

The last lesson ended just as it seemed they could stand no more and before the last blown about sound of the bell faded boys burst from doors like champagne corks, to spew like bubbles down the steps and outside.

Soon a noisy game was in progress and Gabby waited among the dank trees for the gang to arrive and fretted to get started. One by one they came. They were not as timid as last time and, instead of being frightening, the thrashing branches overhead excited the boys as they awaited the final arrival.

It should be Beauty, and Gabby looked forward to having that trusting presence alongside. He at least was someone who wouldn't find fault or cause trouble. But instead he recognized the approaching figure of Whiteyes.

"Let's go!" Whiteyes, after a short pause, looked around once and walked in the direction they had gone last time. The others began to follow. Gabby choked with rage. How he longed to be able to call them back and tell Whiteyes off for trying to usurp the warlord's leadership. The intensity of his fury almost blinded Gabby as he charged past the others and rammed Whiteyes with all the force of his shoulder, knocking him off balance so he fell into a tangle of blackberry vines where he kicked and struggled to tear loose of the thorns.

Gabby, with a look, dared anyone to help his squealing enemy and hustled along another trail hearing the others close behind him. He hoped Whiteyes would die back there or at least get lost and never be seen again. His hopes were dashed when he heard the whining voice. "Hey, wait up." Followed by a monologue of complaints that made Gabby clench his teeth until his jaw ached.

"Don't take us through all these scratchy things eh, Gabby. Yech, it's awful in here."

A step or two of quiet and again Whiteyes' sour tones. "This is a rotten place. Where are them beasts you talked about?" A short pause then, "I should've known this'd be another wild goose chase. Knew all along you were givin' us a line - all those ferocious beasts you saw. You ain't got the guts"

I'll kill him, Gabby screwed his fists tight, one more word and I'll strangle him. 'No,' whispered something deep inside, 'You've got to wait, for Simon and the Unicorn.'

Gabby's hands twisted and clenched and on their own pulled the penknife from his pocket and opened the blade.

"I could do better...Rabbits are about his size of Beast"

The ugly voice tore the last of Gabby's restraint and he whirled, forgetting everything but the necessity to silence it. At the same instant a flailing whirr of wings dashed from under his feet and Gabby's temper turned on the russet pheasant. Like a shot he was after it, the boys yelling and thundering behind him and the pheasant flapping just off the ground. Arrows and stones thudded around it and panic stricken it turned and blundered blindly into its pursuers.

Gabby threw himself on top of it and plunged the penknife again and again into the breast of the struggling, screaming bird. To Gabby the screams were Whiteyes being silenced forever and he stabbed until the eyes glazed. Triumphantly he lifted the still twitching body high by its legs while the boys danced around him.

"Wow, that was great!" Tod flashed the blade of his knife and looked hungrily into the trees. "Let's find something else!"

Whiteyes stood to one side, nervously eyeing Gabby, his face a light shade of green.

Gabby, glowing like a gladiator fresh from the ring, tore feathers from the bird's tail and stuck them in his hair. Then he cleaned his knife in the ground, remembering how good it had felt when he stabbed it into the pheasant's heart, and he was eager to do it again. A fire burned in his chest and its flames spurred him on so, stashing the corpse in the fork of a tree, he plunged eagerly among the shadows that now held fear for neither him nor his followers.

They moved quietly, eyes greedily searching the hollow quiet. A twig snapped. As one they stopped, straining like pointers. A shadow moved and with a whoop The Killers were after it, plunging through or over whatever lay in their path. They noticed neither scratches nor torn clothes, intent only on the fox that dove and twisted ahead of them. Halfway across a clearing a stone struck the side of the red animal's head, bowling it over. It rolled twice and as it struggled to its feet an arrow dove into its side and another quivered from one russet haunch. Panting, the band of boys swarmed over the unconscious creature and picking it up they tossed it into the air again and again while blood splashed over them.

Finally, their squealing frenzy quieted, and Gabby felt the lateness of the hour and knew they must return before lights out. Throwing the fox over his shoulder he led the way back to pick up the pheasant, and then headed schoolward, his gang leaping and shouting around him. Gabby rejoiced at the success this hunt had brought. Even Whiteyes couldn't complain now.

A cold wind reached down, chilling them and carrying shouts from the nearby playing field. It also brought a sudden thought to Gabby who stopped short in his tracks.

"What's up now? Come on, we'll be late supper".

"What's the matter, Gabby?" Everyone was hungry and cold. Weariness ached in their joints and they were eager to relive their conquests in the warmth of their beds.

Gabby pointed out the blood spatters that covered them and then a peat colored pool nearby.

Reluctantly the boys went to the water. They hated to remove the proof of desperate battles and saved spots that were safely hidden under shirtsleeves, cuffs and collars.

Gabby's, however, had begun to feel dry and uncomfortable and they looked like fungus on his skin. He scrubbed to remove every speck, after which he went to the carcasses sprawled on the ground like a couple of empty sacks.

Gabby began to dig under a pine tree, using his knife to break the hard ground, and then his hands. When the grave was big enough, he stuffed pheasant and fox into it and scooped earth back over them. The fox seemed to mock him from under the pheasant's ruffled wing and it seemed to take a long time to hide that grinning mask.

"Hey, what's Gabby doing?" In a rush the boys came and pulled the bodies from their grave. Gabby tried to explain why they couldn't keep them, but no one paid attention to his signs and anger this time, thought of losing their trophies being too much to bear.

From a safe distance Whiteyes goaded them on. "He wants all the glory, that's what. Taking what we won. Come on gang, let's go!" With a triumphant look toward his leader he led the way to the playing field and Gabby stood by the hole watching them go.

Christ, I should have killed him! I should! I should! Gabby banged his head against a tree in frustration. Now we'll all get caught for sure and that'll end everything.

Stupid bastards. One minute he had everyone right where he wanted them, the next they were ready to follow Whiteyes. He'd grown soft, that was it. All that playing with the Unicorn and other critters was teaching different ways that didn't help in the real world. He had to be tough to survive. And he wanted to do more than survive. He wanted to be Somebody. They'd see! He'd make them forget anyone else, once and for all.

The wind was one long hollow sigh and a drop of rain fell. Gabby looked upward and wondered if he should run away now but with all the killing and excitement, he didn't seem to be able to remember where it was he planned to go. He sighed and waited.

171

He ignored the gang when they returned, just sat looking at the sky; but his heart leaped with relief.

"There's no way to hide them," Tod muttered sheepishly. "Whiteyes is stupid."

Gabby felt a rush of satisfaction.

Quietly the corpses were put back into the hole and covered. Gabby cut off the fox's brush and gave it to Tod, then led the way out of the forest.

The rain became heavy causing everyone to run for shelter, and Gabby sneaked upstairs for a shower letting the water beat onto his skin, scrubbing it as the rain did the field outside.

Late that night the gang gathered in Gabby's cubicle. All but Whiteyes who hadn't heard where the meeting was to be held and waited on his bed in lonely exasperation.

It was hard to keep the noise down as everyone wanted to tell his own side of the hunt and they lived it again with appropriate exaggeration. Gabby sat on his bed and swung his legs to protect the gun's hiding place, tomorrow he would talk, he promised himself, it was time.

Tomorrow! Why tomorrow was his birthday! Some people got presents but he never had. Fifteen was a pretty important age to become. He kind of wished someone knew. Perhaps the Unicorn did. Good feelings surged then he remembered his resolve not to go into the wood if he wanted the power he craved. He had to be strong, and tough and mean or his life back on the streets would be hell. A jolt of pain made him blink as imagination pictured the bloody fox's mask looking at him from the grave. He squelched the thought.

"Weren't they, Gabby, eh?" Tod's voice shattered his thoughts and Gabby's head whirled. "Weren't they the fastest critters you ever saw?"

Gabby pulled himself together, nodded vehemently and concentrated on the talk around him.

"Wow, you should have seen the way Gabby stuck that bird, it fighting and flapping like a mad thing. It was about the biggest bird I ever saw and it was my sling shot that turned it toward us."

On and on they talked, and more and more Gabby wished they'd shut up and leave him alone. When they finally did it was with plans to hold a hunt once a week.

Gabby meant to stop Beauty and find out why he'd not been with them that afternoon, but the boy slipped away before he could catch him. Almost as though he didn't want to talk to me, Gabby thought. In fact, he'd been that way for a while now though the gifts still appeared. Weird kid. I could have told him about my birthday. Oh hell! Gabby scrunched up tight. Maybe tomorrow Simon will come.

CHAPTER XXVIII

As forbidden wine to an alcoholic the killings fanned the spark of violence in The Killers, engulfing each with thirst for more. Like wildfire the mood spread so in one day sullen acceptance of authority changed to blatant defiance throughout the school and the staff checked and oiled their guns.

The boys seemed to adopt the traits of the imaginary animals they hunted, prowling the school baiting adults and terrorizing the smaller and weaker among them. Gabby stayed separate from the rest, somehow the bullying he had once enjoyed interested him no longer, but he was excited by the powder keg atmosphere and roamed the corridors rapping the new drumsticks he had whittled. They were a birthday present to himself and he reveled in the glory of being fifteen at last.

At four o clock he raced across the playing field before anyone could stop him, not even taking time for the hidden way behind the shed. If he could he would have shouted for joy as he leaped into the wood.

He bucked like a colt through fallen red and gold leaves. The monkey joined him and together they careened through the trees, spreading their exuberance so other animals joined them, bounding, galloping, hopping.

Stopping at last by a stream Gabby drank and washed away every trace of the outer world then he looked around for the Unicorn. They had usually met by now. Sitting back on his heels he took in all the changes Autumn had brought. Dark evergreens made a background for brilliantly leafed maples, poplar and ash. Gabby scooped up an armful of leaves and showered rustling flames over himself and the monkey. Then they scampered on.

Where was the Unicorn?

On they went. The fur of a black panther dusted Gabby's leg and he looked into the depths of emerald eyes before they blinked out and disappeared. Another green caught his attention as two budgies shivered leaves and sidled up and down a twig watching him first with one eye, then the other. Gabby moved faster. Anxiety creeping in. Already he smelled dusk and he had not yet found his friend.

Urgency pushed him until he was farther into the wood than he had ever been before. A gap in the trees showed him a lake whose surface mirrored the start of a magnificent sunset. Gabby stood among bulrushes and looked with awe at some of the most enormous creatures he had ever seen. They were far away against the opposite bank, but he recognized them from a book at school. The teacher had said they were extinct, but he'd always known teachers didn't know anything.

Noisy quacking announced the arrival of ducks that landed with a rush of webbed feet, leaving long rippling vees behind them. Gabby watched them dive, slide their heads under the surface and rise to shake splashes of sunset from their feathers. He wanted to catch pieces of sunset too and tore off his clothes, leaving them in a crumpled pile as he threw himself among the reds and golds, feeling water cover him like silk. He had never learned to swim but as it did to the wild things it came naturally to him and he looked down into depths where the sun wove skeins, lacing a ladder to the bottom.

Gabby pulled himself onto the bank and sat in reflections of salmon colored sky. The sun sank faster now. Gabby leapt to his feet. The Unicorn! He must find it! He dragged on clothes as he ran beside the lake and then away up a steep rocky track. His feet seemed to know where to go and took him, clambering and sliding over rocks that flashed ruby, emerald, topaz and diamonds. His eyes were dazzled by their brilliance.

The climb was almost perpendicular but suddenly the hill flattened and, on its peak, stood the unicorn, each hair outlined, gilded by the sunset, dipped in its gold. Gabby watched, not wanting to move. It was as though the beautiful creature prayed, so intently it gazed into the last vestiges of the sun. The silence was absolute, and time hung still.

The sun disappeared leaving one crimson streak and nothing moved anywhere.

A lone bird's twitter made Gabby conscious of breathing again and the Unicorn turned its head toward him, its horn glowing as though some sun had been captured there. Gabby ran toward his friend but slowed to a walk sensing a deep and overpowering sadness in the golden eyes that watched him. Usually they danced with life and happiness, and Gabby wondered and felt troubled. The Unicorn's soft muzzle brushed his cheek, breathing a soft caress, and side by side in the velvet darkness they watched the huge moon and listened to the singing of the stars.

Gabby brimmed with tears until a great lake of sorrow filled him, but he didn't know why.

The hoot of an owl announced how late it was but the thought of returning to school frightened Gabby. It was as though a crowd of evil things waited and reminding himself, he was now fifteen didn't help at all. Gabby pressed his cheek hard against the Unicorn and twined his fingers into the soft beautiful mane as though to tie himself to it forever.

With the nudge Gabby knew so well the Unicorn insisted he go and for a moment they looked into each other's eyes. Gabby fought desperately against the belief that he saw goodbye not just for now but forever. Gently the Unicorn pulled away and broke into a long floating stride that carried it soundlessly over the rocks.

A sweep of heavy tail left a haze of sparkles, and then there was only darkness. Gabby stood too heavy in his heart to move.

A pressure against his leg drew his attention to the little monkey who huddled against him. Reaching down Gabby took its leathery hand and lifted it. The warm presence against his neck comforted him as he started back down the hill over rocks that now smoldered in their own fires. Fireflies led the way as far as the wood's edge where their lights went out- and then the monkey bit him. Shocked Gabby swiped at it, knocking it to the ground, where it snarled at him, showing its sharp teeth before fleeing back into the Wood.

Gabby felt blood running down his neck as he stepped alone into the blackness of the playing field to stand under a miserly moon serenaded by one bored cricket. Tears flooded his throat and, horrified by this weakness he had never felt before, he waited until the spell was over. I'll be back tomorrow he told himself. Tomorrow. Tomorrow. It became a chant in his mind as he walked toward the dark building.

The meaning of the darkness seeped through to him. Everyone was in bed. His absence was sure to have been noticed. What excuse could he make? Clouds closed around the small patch of brightness where the moon had been. A wind made him tighten and hunch against its bite. A cough floated from an open window.

When Gabby tried the front door, it was locked and remembering all the bolts inside he wasted no time but went around to the kitchen. This door also stayed solid against his push. He stood back, thinking and shivering. The windows were too small and high for him to hit with a pebble in hopes of alerting one of the gang. He huddled against the wall where he and Simon had once sheltered from the rain and his eyes fell on the garbage cans. He went to one and felt inside until he found the slim metal of a tin lid. Confident, he kneeled in front of the door and slipped it into the crack feeling for the lock's obstruction, concentrating, aware of nothing but the searching tin.

"What…"

Gabby whirled and was blinded by bright light.

"You!" Recognition seemed to bring pleasure to the guard who loomed a black shape. "You little bastard. Well I've got you now and soon you'll be sorry you ever saw my face. After what you did to me, I should put you six feet under!"

Gabby cursed his luck and hid his fear.

"Take that smart look off your face or I'll do it for you, you…"

Automatically Gabby's hand flew up to ward off the blow, and the forgotten can lid he held slashed deep into the man's palm.

Swearing, he stuffed the wound into his mouth, his rage a palpable thing that intensified and throbbed in the darkness. The frustration and fury of eight months overflowed and with a thundering whack to the side of Gabby's head he sent him tumbling amid clattering cans. The noise of colliding metal joined with pain and before any of it stopped Gabby felt himself hoisted by his collar and dragged into the storage shed nearby.

The door clicked shut and he struggled to escape the solid hunk of flesh that held him. Kicking, biting, punching. He was thrown against the wall and spun again to face his attacker. The flashlight lay on the floor sending light to pool on the ceiling, only slightly illuminating the nightmare shape that slowly removed the belt from its trousers.

It seemed inhuman and like a cornered rat Gabby attacked, but the belt burned across his face, throwing him backward. He scrambled forward and felt it cut his chest and sting along his shoulder. Like a machine the arm rose and fell, and Gabby scrambled into a corner to hunker with face between his knees, arms protecting his head. The belt with its wicked silver buckle came down again and again, and Gabby became more conscious of sound than of pain. Slam, as it hit him, the sibilant whistle as it cut through the air, and the hoarse bubbling breath of the man. Gabby's nose filled with the smell of sweat and, as his body became numb, back rage grew and grew until it was almost too big for his slight frame to hold. Each crashing thud branded it deeper into his soul until the tumult faded into the distance.

CHAPTER XXIX

Gabby awoke to the smell of sacking under his cheek, and when he lifted his head pain leapt alive all over his body. Light was just seeking its way through the one smudgy window and illuminated the rust colored patches that stuck his shirt and trouser legs to his body. Gingerly he touched his swollen cheek and inspected the cuts and bruises on his hands and wrists. But the older bite from the monkey hurt more than any. He reeled to a corner and vomited.

Back on the sacks Gabby shivered and wondered what would happen next.

Bitterness grew and filled him. It was like a once familiar companion returned after an absence, fitting back into its bed stronger than before.

Clattering came from the kitchen, but no one came near. Gabby walked stiffly to the window and was surprised to see that sunshine warmed the spilled garbage outside. He looked for a way to escape but the window was too small, and the solid door bolted on the outside. The shed was empty except for the pile of sacks, a watering can hanging on a hook, and some withered leaves that had once been lettuce. There was nothing to do but wait.

Gabby found it necessary to use one corner of the room for a toilet. As morning wore on the shed grew hot and smelly, and thirst dried his mouth, bringing mirage sounds of water. He slipped into half-dreams where icy streams ran down his throat and his face was submerged in a lake from which he drank and drank.

Sounds brought him painfully to the window through which he saw Cook righting the garbage cans, muttering angrily as he did so. Gabby rapped the glass with his knuckles, but they were too bruised to knock hard enough so he looked around for something better as he licked their pain.

The watering can! Quickly he removed the sprinkler head and rapped the spout briskly against the glass. This time Cook heard and came questioningly toward the shed. His face filled the tiny window and his eyes bugged with surprise to see Gabby. He left and hurried into the building.

It seemed a very long time before anyone else came and Gabby decided Cook had forgotten about him. He'd probably die here! Suddenly the shed looked like a tomb and he smashed the window to let in a surge of fresh air. At least he wouldn't suffocate.

When footsteps finally did approach, Gabby stationed himself opposite the door and stuffed his hands into his pockets. He took them out, crossed his arms instead, then put them back again and, standing on one leg, leaned against the wall.

Two men stood in the sudden brightness of the open door. "Phew! It stinks in here," said the warden's voice.

"I mean who knows what the little bastard was up to." The guard was obviously intent on finishing what he had been saying outside and Gabby stiffened to hear that hated voice. "Like I say, he attacked me with a knife, lurking there in the dark." He held out a hand for Warden to see and Gabby half smiled at the size of the gash.

The guard's voice rose belligerently. "Kids like this ought to be got rid of. Even if he can't talk, he's still leader of the other punks." The voice grew soft, coaxing. "Couldn't he just disappear? No one would ever know the difference. We could say he..."

"I won't have talk like that." Warden spun on his heel and went outside. "We're not lawless. We have a job to do and if you're too scared to do it you shouldn't be here. I don't want you to touch this boy again, you hear? Now get this place cleaned out, feed the kid and take him to the washroom twice a day when everyone's out of the way. More often if he needs it. A week's solitary will cool him down and if I know gangs, they'll have found another leader by then."

The door slammed shut and sounds of talking faded.

Gabby's heart was at the bottom of his stomach. A week! It might as well be forever. That last sentence of Warden's made him go cold, of course it wasn't true. The Killers were faithful to him. Look at all he'd done for them.

But deep inside Gabby remembered how easily they'd followed Whiteyes in the forest even though they'd come back to him in the end. He knew they were faithful to no one and at the excited pitch they were in now they weren't going to wait for anyone. He had to get out of here!

He rushed at the door and kicked it, surprised when it flew open, but the flash of hope died as cook handed him a shovel, some papers and a bag. "Clean the place up, then I'll bring you something to eat."

Again, blank wood faced him and Gabby turned away, weighed down with misery. He cleaned up the filthy corner; almost vomiting in the process. Then Cook returned with a tray from which Gabby grabbed the glass of water and gulped it down, holding it out for more. Cook grumbled but left to bring back a jug from which Gabby drank glass after glass. His spirits rose as his belly filled and as he sat alone in the dimness, he realized that it didn't matter what the gang did. Tonight, the Unicorn would rescue him and of course would keep him with it in the wood forever. He just knew it.

The bread he gnawed tasted good now and his body didn't hurt as much. Strengthened, he paced, pausing each time he passed the window to see if night was coming.

It took a long time but when it did Gabby pressed close to the broken glass, feeling the cold air on his cheek as he watched for the glowing appearance of his rescuer. Any minute it would be here. But of course, it must wait until everyone had gone to bed.

Perhaps the staffroom light was still on. He must be patient.

Gabby's heart beat quick, light strokes of anticipation and his fingers pressed whitely on the wood frame.

When dawn came, he was still there and when he heard rattling sounds from the kitchen he turned and numbly curled up on the sack pulling the blanket they had given him over his head.

He dragged through the second day, thinking only of this night when the Unicorn was sure to come. Again, his eyes strained through darkness and he brushed away the first tiny seed of doubt. In the small hours he heard wolves howl but never the sound of a light stepping hoof. At first song of a waking bird Gabby turned away, cold and disillusioned, to lie thinking bitter thoughts.

The third night Gabby waited for a while and then he knew the Unicorn didn't care. He'd been made a fool of again. Nothing would ever care about him. Same as Simon. He wasn't coming either. What an idiot he'd been to ever think he would after the way he'd made it so Gabby couldn't work with him and the rabbits anymore. Maybe the Unicorn had planned this too! Gabby sat among the old sacks and cobwebs, smelling the dirt he had lived in all his life. He didn't pay any attention to the hair that fell across his eyes or the snot that ran from his nose, just stared unseeingly ahead, biting his lip until he tasted blood.

He sat that way until morning and then well into the day. His insides felt bruised and this inner damage didn't heal but grew worse. In the dark of the fourth hopeless night he ground his face into the sacking and wept.

Next morning, hollow as a dried gourd, Gabby stayed curled up, not touching the food brought him. He lay staring at the wall and it wasn't until noon that thoughts began to seep into his emptiness, and they were all hard and ugly. For the rest of the day and night he roiled with desire for revenge.

When a soft whistle sounded at his window that fifth day it took a moment before Gabby realized what it was. "Gosh Gabby, I've been looking for you everywhere." The whisper swam across the room. "Whiteyes said you'd gone into the other side of the wood and been eaten. Says he saw you go. You sure look awful! Do they torture you?"

Sight of Beauty's face snapped Gabby back to the gang and all it meant to him. His thoughts scrambled remembering how careless he had been entering the Wood that last day and he could almost hear Whiteyes reporting him to the guard who would most want to catch him. Gabby went to the window wanting to hear more.

"Whiteyes called a meeting for tonight. Figures he's Warlord now, but I knew you were somewhere. I'll tell them all. I gotto go. Be back tomorrow -and Gabby- I'm sure glad you're not eaten." A nervous rush and the window was empty. Gabby thought about what he would do to Whiteyes when he got out, of what he would do to anyone who ever got in his way again. He felt a good fifteen now, or maybe even fifty. It had taken a lot of learning but now he knew what to do.

The night was long and he imagined the Killers meeting hoping Beauty got them to believe him. It was cold, with a line of frost blurring the building and Gabby paced in an effort to get warm. He pushed the unyielding door and fretted to be rid of these four ugly walls. Just two more days, but they seemed like years.

As soon as daylight straggled around the clouds he watched for Beauty and when he finally arrived around noon, he looked gaunt and unhappy. First, he pushed a couple of candy bars into Gabby's eager hands and while Gabby ate them Beauty told about the meeting.

"I told them about you but at first they wouldn't believe me. Whiteyes said I was just trying to make trouble, and then they wouldn't let me talk. They're all excited about the hunt that's scheduled for full moon which is soon. Whiteyes said he's going to lead them and show them lots of killing." Suddenly Beauty's eyes were wet and his lips trembled. He looked down. "Whiteyes said bad things about you. Said you were queer because he saw me go to your cubicle."

Gabby knew there was worse to come as Beauty choked and his voice rose to a wail. "I told him about the gun, Gabby, weeks ago. I had to. He beat me up and said he'd blind me with a needle he had. I think he's got it now. He bragged he had a better weapon than anyone else for the next hunt. Oh Gabby, I'm sorry!"

Gabby just looked at him and thought how he'd lost everything he'd worked for. And to top it all Whiteyes had the gun. He

183

remembered the bruises on Beauty's face. He'd forgotten to ask about them.

Beauty left, a small dejected figure swallowed by the shadow of the building, and Gabby stared after him, unseeing.

Damn everything! He kicked the blanket from one end of the room to the other and threw the watering can at the door. Then he pounded the pile of sacks until his arm ached and his fists bled.

That night and the next he watched the moon grow toward fullness, but it still had a few nights to go. Then the seventh day came and in the evening the guard opened the door for the last time and ordered Gabby to his cubicle.

Everyone was in bed although a few curtains twitched as he passed. When he reached his cubicle Gabby immediately fell to his knees and groped for the loose board. Lifting it the cavity beneath glared at him like an empty eye socket. He lowered and raised the board again hoping he'd seen wrong, but the gun was definitely gone.

CHAPTER XXX

No one is more quickly despised than the strong leader in whom weakness is perceived. Gabby found that out when he entered the washroom next morning. After the first expressions of surprise at his appearance eyes blanked over and faces turned away. He clenched his fists and pretended not to notice but it hurt.

Downstairs he was studiously ignored, only Beauty came up full of guilt and sympathy and Gabby knocked him aside, inwardly cursing the boy for being the cause of all his trouble. Gabby lived in a tent of bitterness and when he saw The Killers crowd around Whiteyes he felt impotent to defend himself. Instead he planned vengeance but first there was something important that must be done.

Breakfast over, he pushed roughly through the mob and ran upstairs straight toward the washroom. Once inside he closed the door behind him and strode to the middle where he faced into the shower stall. Sweat broke out on his upper lip and he took a deep breath and coughed. A breath, contraction of the muscles at the base of his throat and Gabby shouted his name as loud as he could. A hoarse rasping bleat bounced back from the white wall in front of him. Trembling he tried again. Nothing. He couldn't believe it and he tried again and again but no voice came and no words formed.

Weakly Gabby sank to the floor. He'd always believed he could talk if he wanted to. Being dumb made him different and kind of

185

spooked the others 'cause they always wondered what was going on inside. It made it fun to fool them. He planned on shocking them all one day with his great roaring secret; his voice puny and young no longer. But now. What about his plans to tell everyone about Whiteyes' lies and see his face fall to hear him? What about all the orders he was going to shout? Despairingly Gabby pleaded with the small distorted boy in the showerhead who stared dumbly back at him. It wasn't fair! Gabby's hand reached for a cake of soap and flung it at the gleaming metal, blotting the weakling figure from its shine. Then Gabby ran from stall to stall turning taps. Basins, baths, showers all gushed, filling the room with steam and then he ran out and down the hall to his cubicle not noticing the boys he collided with on his way.

For a long time, he sat on his bed and slowly his spirits fought back and his ego grew whole again. Hell, he could get by without talking. Hadn't he gotten to be Warlord without it? What was wrong with his fists and tough fighting body? He could still write, couldn't he? Yeah, he'd show everyone who was boss and rub Whiteyes' nose in it before he got rid of him for good. It didn't matter now if he was sent back to prison or even hanged, so long as he did a good job on Whiteyes first, and anyone else who let him down.

Gabby combed his hair high, put on his most ferocious expression and clumped downstairs.

That night the moon was just a sliver away from full and Gabby heard the almost inaudible scuffles as The Killers gathered below him in Whiteyes cubicle.

He patted a last layer of dust on the whisker line of his chin and admired the swollen cheek and half-closed eye that made him look more vicious than anything he could do artificially. Then he crept to Whiteyes' curtain and whisked it aside. A gasp met his appearance. He strode over the sitting boys, flesh or floor it made no difference, and handed Tod a sheet of paper. Then he left.

After a moment he sneaked back close enough to make sure his note was being read aloud. He relaxed as he heard Tod's voice. "If you believe the lies of a turd like Whiteyes and go with him tomorrow you deserve the hunt you'll get. Mud, more nettles, and probably getting lost and attacked. Tomorrow at midnight I shall go to a place I know full of good things to eat and water better than soda pop. There are no swamps or brambles but bigger animals than you've ever seen. If you come with me, you'll kill beasts grown men would pay money for. If you have guts, follow me. If you're cowards go with Whiteyes." Tod's voice stopped and no one said a word.

Gabby silently crept away. Surely that would get them. There was nothing else he could do so he slept... and tossed and dreamed.

A huge red sun rose over the Wood and as it climbed it burned each tree it touched. Gabby stood in the field outside the school and watched the fire come closer and closer. He heard the roar and a crackling like pistol shots. Birds fell from the sky like shooting stars and like sparks others flew out of the burning trees uttering small screams. The fire reached the edge of the clearing and Gabby pressed his palms to his eyes to protect them from the searing heat. Just when he felt he would burn and shrivel the sun changed to an enormous glowing moon. It was very close and hung over the black skeletal spars of the wood. As he watched the moon melted into a waterfall of tears that fell with a great sobbing sound to the ground. Gabby was swept off his feet and hurled along on the current, tossed and buffeted by the force of it.

He awoke trembling and confused.

Morning arrived bright eyed and alert. It was one of those clear days when the world seems full of space and sounds carry a long way. The knot in the pit of Gabby's stomach grew bigger as time progressed although he acted as though he had nothing on his mind but what he was doing that very moment. He ignored everyone, making it plain he needed none of them and from the corner of his eye he saw Beauty always hovering like a whipped dog.

Calmly he ate the evening meal and, looking at no one, wandered nonchalantly up to bed. Once behind his curtain he gave way to worry. What if nobody came? What if Whiteyes used more lies and won them his way? One minute. Gabby knew they'd follow him, the next he filled with doubts.

Finally clinging to the positive he thought about the terrific hunt he'd show them. Why, they'd plead with him to be Warlord after it and look up to him like a god. No one would ever be able to undermine his authority again! Already he heard the gang's praises.

And while they hunt beasts tonight, I'll hunt Whiteyes. I'll finish him off but good and he'll go knowing I've won. The thought brought a triumphant thrill with it.

The moon lit his cubicle brightly and he stood on his bed to look out. As he faced the wood his lips curled in a tight smile. Now you'll be sorry for making a game of me, you lousy Unicorn. And Simon. I'll show you I don't care what happens to you anymore than you do me. I'm Warlord of The Killers and I don't need either of you.

Fakers all of them! Gabby pulled the partially packed bag from behind his bed and dumped the contents onto the blanket. His eyes fastened on the pouch that held his old drum- sticks. He picked it up and dropped it through the bars of his window, hearing a faraway plop as it landed. Stupid broken sticks. Why ever had he kept them?

Suddenly he remembered the guards. It would be awful if they stayed awake tonight of all nights and no one could get past! Quickly he scurried to the top of the stairs and looked down. Two men played cards at the bottom. One yawned and stretched. "Sure you don't mind being left alone? A night's sleep sounds awful good to me right now."

"Hell," the other answered. "They don't need two of us Not while I've got this anyway." He tapped the gun at his side. "Don't let on to Warden though."

"Right. G'night then."

Gabby watched the one leave and saw the other slouch toward the kitchen with his coffee cup. He heard him talk to Cook and the voice grew louder as the guard started back. "Bake something good then. See you later."

Gabby turned around and leaned his back against the bars of the banister. Damn cook had to decide to bake tonight! Usually everyone liked the good smells and anticipation of muffins for breakfast but, oh Christ, not tonight! Gabby's heart sank to his toes, but a sudden idea jolted him to his feet and sent him at a silent lope to Beauty's cubicle. He ignored the wan face that lit up when it recognized him and scribbled something quickly on his pad, holding it in a dap of moonlight under Beauty's nose.

The boy read and as he did happiness fled from his eyes leaving them empty and desolate. "Oh Gabby, please don't make me. You know I'll do anything for you but that. I hate them all so."

Gabby took hold of the scrawny shoulder and dug pain into it with all the strength of his fingertips.

Beauty sighed, sagged with despair, and whispered so it could barely be heard. "Okay, Gabby."

With a curt nod Gabby left. In a short while he heard the stair creak and smiled with satisfaction to know Cook would be out of the way by midnight and with any luck the guard would drink himself into a stupor as he usually did when alone.

Fleetingly Gabby wondered if Beauty had planned to come with him, then he concentrated on polishing his penknife and listening to the slow half hours strike.

CHAPTER XXXI

Gabby's heart seemed to beat in unison to the twelve shuddering strokes of midnight and for a moment he thought it also stopped at the same moment as the clock's chime. Pulling himself together he licked dry lips and crept along the hall. When he saw the guard asleep with his head on the table, he breathed a sigh of relief and padded downstairs, leaning over the man for a moment. Alcohol blew forth on soft snores and Gabby moved on, satisfied.

The dark passage funneled him into the kitchen where a clutter of doughy bowls caught moonlight in their hollows. Panic fluttered for an instant as his hand found no key in the oven still warm from prematurely halted baking, but almost immediately he spotted it on the counter alongside and quickly opened the door. He paused. The building was alive with muffled creaks as of an army on the move. Were they coming to follow him or to go with Whiteyes? He'd soon know.

Gabby ran full speed into the night, his breath a white companion on the frosty air. He didn't allow himself to look back until he reached the wood and then he saw the figures darting after him. His heart pounded triumphantly as silent boys gathered around him. Whiteyes stared malevolently from the outskirts. Only one gang member was missing and Gabby's glance touched the lone light that burned at the back of the building. Well, Beauty probably didn't like hunting anyway.

Beckoning, Gabby plunged into the wood and heard mutters from those behind as sweet warm air soothed their shivering. As he paused to get his bearings the rest looked about at the alien beauty and its strangeness made them uncomfortable and stirred feelings they didn't understand. They shuffled uneasily and crowded together.

"What's that funny smell?" whispered one.

"Flowers. Maybe roses," someone answered. "It's weird in here."

Gabby felt familiar gentle stirrings and quickly shook his head, spat, and smashed a toadstool with his foot. Then he ripped a bracken spear from the ground and hurled it into the trees ahead.

Returned to feelings they understood the Killers followed his example and soon a barrage of spears whistled through the air. One crumpled a spider's web and its occupant was crushed beneath eager feet. Three sunflowers fell, snapped like brittle bones and the pack panted behind their leader, fired with expectation.

At the rear Whiteyes fondled something that swung heavily in his jacket pocket and smiled as he watched the bounding figure of Gabby ahead.

Suddenly a young antelope stood in their path, eyes full of moonbeams. Recognizing its human friend, it tossed its head and bounded forward to play. Gabby stopped short, the boys cannoning into him. They saw the animal and knocked Gabby aside yelling and brandishing their weapons as they charged. Uncomprehending, the antelope waited until they were almost upon it, then wheeled and bolted. Stabbing the ground with sharp hooves it ran blindly from the uproar, bewilderment changing to terror.

The gang tore through unresisting brush, every sense intent on their quarry. Clumps of moss flew and branches broke under flailing arms. Gabby ran too, caught in the current and spurred by noise that crashed around his head and filled the wood.

Panting and drained by fear the young antelope stopped, unable to run farther and turned to face its pursuers. A rock hit between its eyes, chasing the light from them as it sank to its knees. As one the boys were upon it stabbing, striking, each wanting his share in the death and when they stood back there were few hairs of the once sleek coat that were not drowned in blood.

Breathing hard, eyes bright and elated, the boys looked to Gabby for more. The power of Warlord was his again and Whiteyes stood apart, mouth tight, forgotten.

The gang eagerly pressed on, pushing Gabby into the lead, not one giving a last look at the antelope dead in the thicket where it had been born only that spring. Eyes honed for the slightest movement, the boys strained forward, blood lust flooding each cell.

No barriers hindered the marauding feet that left a trampled swathe of ruin behind them. An owl toppled from its perch with an arrow through its breast, a parrot fell with a shattered wing and each boy who stepped over it pulled a bright feather to stick in his shirt. Gabby ran on, not allowing himself to think other than that he had won the leadership he had craved for so long and his fame would spread back to the streets where all would look up to him when he returned.

Needing rest, the panting boys left the body of the ocelot whose dead green eyes still stared and flung themselves down to drink from a stream.

"Wow, that's good!" Pirate wiped his face. "This is some place. Gabby, you really done us proud."

The others grunted appreciatively, and Gabby looked around at them, exulting. But he wasn't done yet. He'd make this time something they'd never forget. He'd be known as the Warlord above all Warlords.

Pleased to recognize where they were, he led the way to a nearby clearing, broke a hefty branch from an apple tree and using it as a club smashed the wood of a hollow log. It fell open showing waxen combs of glistening honey.

"Hey, look out! Bees!" Tod yelled.

Everyone ran to a safe distance and turned to see Gabby close his fingers over one in his hand and crush it. As he did the same to more he grinned, showing unscathed palms. He broke off honeycomb and poured thick nectar into his mouth.

"They don't sting! Come on guys, let's eat!" Tod was first back and soon everyone guzzled sweetness while Gabby watched, benevolent provider of their feast.

Gorged, the boys lay on their backs and looked into the eye of the moon.

"You know something?" Fang's voice floated dreamily. "This is the place Gabby used to tell us about, with all the beasts. We thought he made it up, but it was real."

"We're darn lucky to have a Warlord like Gabby. How many people are brave enough to explore a place like this all by themselves?"

Other words of praise rose, and Gabby thrilled to hear them. This'll sure be riling Whiteyes, he thought.

As though reading his mind Whiteyes spat and stood up. He stuck his thumbs in his belt and stood over them all. "Yeah, but all he's showed us is smaller stuff. Where's the king beast I want to know. That's what I want to get."

All eyes turned to Gabby.

"He said we'd hunt the biggest and best beast in the forest." Whiteyes' voice was like a bad smell in the air. "I bet even Gabby's scared to kill that one."

Jarring as a slipped cog the words rocked Gabby's pleasure and his thoughts tumbled.

"Oh shut up, Whitey, I bet that's where he's taking us next. Aren't you, Gabby?" Fang waited expectantly.

Fleetingly Gabby saw the image of the Unicorn and felt again hurt and anger at its desertion when he'd needed it. Instead it had made him soft, had nearly lost him everything he had fought for for so many years. *Well I got rid of Simon and the rabbits who tried the same thing, now the Unicorn will get what it deserves too and that pig Whiteyes will never be able to accuse me of being chicken!* The decision made, Gabby felt suddenly strong and all-powerful and he jumped up, setting off with a determined stride.

Eagerly everyone sprang to follow, pushing to be first. They prowled soundlessly over pine needles, then rustled through piles of bright leaves. At the edge of a lake Gabby halted and pointed up to a moon-painted bluff.

He hurried on. Soon it would be over, and his supremacy established once and for all. His pulse pounded in his ears. He didn't feel water soak his feet as he splashed across a finger of lake, breaking down bulrushes and setting adrift waterlilies with his tearing stride.

They began to climb and a tingle passed from boy to boy. It was as though they smelled their victim and they began to whisper the chant of their game. "Killers kill, Killers kill." It matched the rhythm of their feet clumping like jackboots over the increasingly rocky ground.

A white shape moved in the shadows. Gabby stopped and felt the breath of those behind hot on his neck. Traitorous Unicorn! He flung himself forward and a yell came from the roots of each boy's being. Gabby was first on the beast, knife drawn, fire burning his veins. All the disappointments and despair of his life rode the blade that stabbed blindly up and down, killing the Unicorn and all the others who betrayed him.

"That's no beast."

The words penetrated the blood haze of his mind and pulling away he saw before him the frail heap of an old man. Gabby stared unbelieving at the blood smeared white smock. Slowly, dreading, his eyes travelled to Simon's face where the gentle eyes looked at him through their pain and very low his lips murmured, "Oh Gabby, Gabby, I came for you..."

A flutter of breath and Simon was gone. Gabby couldn't move. He wanted to die.

Voices behind him sounded a million miles away and vaguely he heard someone say, "Come on, let's go. He was just an old man no one wanted anyway."

All Gabby understood was a voice deep inside that said, "He came for me. He did come." It didn't matter when Whiteyes told the others to follow him. "Come on, we don't need Gabby, he showed us the way. Killers kill. Killers kill." The chant started, others picked it up and, regaining the excited tempo of before it drew farther away.

Gabby crouched alone, looking at the beautiful old face, pleading for it not to have happened. A dry sob tore through him, seeming to rend his soul until it was as raw and bleeding as the body before him.

Something landed on his shoulder and jolted him back into the moonlit night. Furry arms clutched his neck and the monkey chattered frantically into his ear. Beyond Gabby heard the sound of distant chanting and sudden realization of what it meant filled him with horror. Bounding to his feet he tore up the hillside in a sobbing desperate run. He went straight up, not looking for trails, and he slipped and slid over rocks, pushing frantically through bushes. His lungs gasped for air and the monkey clung tightly, leaning forward like a wizened jockey.

The rock became so steep Gabby scrabbled on hands and knees. He clawed and pulled with his fingers, body numb beyond pain. He seemed to move in an interminable nightmare, and always his eyes remained fixed on the summit above him. Sweat and tears ran down his face, but he noticed neither. For an instant he held his breath to listen. The chanting came from below. There was hope and he lunged on, sound drowned by his own gasping sobs.

He burst onto the bald crest of the hill as the first ray of sun lit the Unicorn who faced him, and his whole being cried out with love for it and begged forgiveness from the gentle golden eyes.

There was no time. Shouts of hunters filled the air and their crashing progress was too close. Gabby spun to face the sound, arms up as a futile barrier, mouth open in a soundless scream. The monkey still rode high on his shoulders, rigid with fear as a storm of stones hurtled toward them. One hit Gabby's temple and he stumbled but quickly scrambled upright. He had to stop them! He had to!

An explosion deafened him and somehow his legs wouldn't work. He struggled but it was no use and he felt the ground beneath his hands. Still he fought the uselessness of his body until, through a strange fog, he saw that the boys had stopped and backed away, staring at him. He had won! It was finished, he could forget them all now and stay with the Unicorn who stood over him. Everything was all right.

A lone cuckoo called and Gabby's eyes drifted to the glowing cloud of mane. He reached toward it and his hand fell softly back to the ground holding a long shimmering strand.

CHAPTER XXXII

"You killed Gabby! Why the hell did you kill him?" Tod shouted and everyone looked in horror at Whiteyes who still held the gun as if not knowing what to do with it.

Whiteyes flinched at the accusation in their eyes and answered defensively. "I thought he was the monster. How could I tell with that monkey sitting on his shoulder and the sun glaring and all? It wasn't my fault."

The boys left him and looked at Gabby who lay between the hooves of the strange animal as though asleep in the morning sunshine. Each felt surprise at how young and gentle he looked and wondered where all his fierceness had gone. Why had they all been so afraid of him? They looked and saw themselves lying there and were afraid. Wordlessly, avoiding each other's eyes, they walked slowly back down the hill.

Whiteyes threw the gun behind a rock and wondered what had gone wrong.

The Unicorn whinnied softly, calling Gabby to waken and gently nudging him as he had done so often before. Again, it whinnied, and wheeled to canter away, spinning around and tossing its head, but Gabby did not join the game. Once more the Unicorn called, a quiet broken sound, then slowly returned, head hanging, and stood motionless.

Word travelled quickly throughout the wood and the animals came. Wolf, bear, lions, snakes and birds they all mourned for the boy they had accepted as their own.

The elephant lifted the feather-light body and laid it carefully over the Unicorn's back where blood dripped down the white flanks, marking a trail to the meadow to which they gently carried him.

The Unicorn kneeled and gently eased the body onto the grass.

Gray wolves dug Gabby's grave and after a while the meadow was empty except for a small sorrowing monkey and the white Unicorn whose coat was to remain dull and stained through many rains to come.

EPILOGUE

The experiment had failed. Two yellow buses were taken from their shed and filled again with boys for the long drive back to remand homes and prisons of civilization. Gabby, presumed to have run away by the authorities, was soon forgotten except by the wan pretty boy who mourned him.

The school had not been empty long when the helicopter flew in and Joe and Tony got out to dismantle the generator and pick up a few things that were left. The building already looked abandoned and the two men felt depressed as they worked.

Joe looked across at the gently rustling trees of the wood and sighed to see the path of crushed ferns that led into it. He walked over and picked up an arrow with a broken tip. Further on he saw a row of broken sunflowers. As he looked into the peaceful greenness, he whispered to himself. "I'm sorry. I'm sorry we ever built the damn place!"

Tony came up beside him. "They won't hurt it anymore. Let's go."

As the helicopter swung away Joe looked down into the wood below and saw something flash as it bounded across a green meadow. "I could swear I saw a horse down there Tony."

"Aw come on, you'll be seeing Unicorns next."

But both men watched the speck for as long as they possibly could.

The End

Made in the
USA
Middletown, DE